Ordeal at
Iron Mountain

The Eagle Wings Series

Ordeal at Iron Mountain

Linda Rae Rao

Fleming H. Revell
A Division of Baker Book House Co
Grand Rapids, Michigan 49516

© 1995 by Linda Rae Rao

Published by Fleming H. Revell
a division of Baker Book House Company
P.O. Box 6287, Grand Rapids, MI 49516-6287

Printed in the United States of America

Library of Congress Cataloging-in-Publication Data

Rao, Linda Rae.
    Ordeal at Iron Mountain / Linda Rae Rao.
        p. cm. — (Eagle wings series)
    ISBN 0-8007-5568-5
    1. United States—History—Revolution, 1775–1783—Fiction.
2. Cherokee Indians—Fiction. I. Title. II. Series. III. Series: Rao,
Linda Rae, 1943–   Eagle wings.
    PS3568.A5957073   1995
    813'.54—dc20   95-14311

To Mom and Poppy
As parents and grandparents,
they stand as loving examples
to all who know them

Acknowledgments

For this, the second book of the Eagle Wings Series, I must again thank my family for their continuing loving support and encouragement; and as always, my agent, Helen Hosier, who continues to work on my behalf.

In addition to these, I wish to convey my thanks to Mr. Bill Petersen and all of those people at Revell who have worked so diligently to produce this book in its final form. There are two other people, in particular, I must thank by name. Becky VanArragon, the in-house editor who was so extremely helpful in preparing the manuscript for *Eagles Flying High*, has been a delight to work with on this book as well. What a wonderful discovery to find an editor on the same wavelength. Her considerate, helpful attitude along with her editorial expertise has played an important part in the production of these two books.

Finding one editor with whom you have a good rapport is wonderful. Finding two is fantastic. From the moment Anna Wilson Fishel first called to discuss the manuscript for this second book, I knew immediately that it was in expert hands. What a joy it was to see the great care and craftsmanship with which she directed the polishing of this work.

Last, but not least, I wish to thank Howard Walker for his patience in answering a multitude of horse-related questions over the past few years. I have loved horses ever since my uncle put me up on his farm horse when I was four years old. So it was a long-held dream come true when we bought our first horse. The person from whom we bought our second horse four years ago directed us to Howard, considered by many as The Farrier Par Excellence. He has not only taken excellent care of our horses' feet over the past four years, he has become our friend, sharing a keen interest in history, especially surrounding Native Americans. He has been a source of valuable information and has taught us a great deal about caring for our animals. In spite of a busy schedule, he has always been graciously willing to take time to answer all of our questions without ever making us feel foolish for asking. I wish everyone who has horses had someone like Howard Walker around to help take proper care of these magnificent creatures.

Prologue

A cold winter rain drummed against the leaded glass panes of the library windows of Canfield Manor. Inside a roaring fire blazed in the hearth as two men settled comfortably in the large easy chairs drawn close to the warmth.

"I must say, Canfield, that was a delightful meal, and this brandy is the finest I've had the pleasure to taste in a very long time." The speaker sipped his crystal glass of after-dinner brandy. "I hope you'll not take offense by my curiosity, but you haven't mentioned anything more about this job you have in mind. Quite frankly, I'm wondering what an accomplished actor like myself can possibly do for a man of your lofty social standing who has no connection whatsoever with the theater."

"No offense taken, Crane. I can understand your curiosity. If you'll bear with me for a few moments, I'd like to tell you a story.

"There were once two brothers who were orphaned while very young. Two uncles and an aunt survived. The boys were separated. One child was cared for by one of the uncles and eventually taken to the American colonies. The other was taken in by the aunt and remained here in England.

"Fortunately for the boys, both families were very well situated. The brother who stayed in England enjoyed a pampered childhood and inherited a substantial estate that, unfortunately, has dwindled in recent years due to a rather extended run of bad luck at the gaming tables." Canfield cleared his throat and straightened the ruffles on his shirt before continuing.

Emory Crane listened intently.

"The other brother also enjoyed the luxuries of life in the colonies on a large plantation he inherited from his deceased uncle. Unfortunately, this brother couldn't adjust to the rebellious attitude of the colonials and in his effort to remain faithful to the king, fell victim to that rabble and was killed."

"That's a sad story," Crane commented, still waiting for Canfield's point. "Except not so sad for the other brother in England if he stands to inherit the American estate."

Crane's host studied him sternly for a long silent moment, and the actor decided that he must watch his tongue. It had been a long time between acting jobs and no matter what he had heard about Canfield's reputation, he could use the handsome salary he had been promised for his assistance.

Canfield's glare softened slightly into a smile that was not exactly reassuring; nevertheless, he continued. "That does seem logical, doesn't it? However, the second uncle had also immigrated to the colonies and built up an equally impressive estate. This estate should rightfully have gone to his grandson and, upon the grandson's tragic death, to the surviving brother in England."

"Should have?" Crane asked, slightly confused by the growing complications of the story.

"I see the story is getting away from you," Canfield observed as he finished the last of his brandy. "I'll get to the point. I am the brother in England. My brother, Bradford Keene, was adopted by our uncle, Lord John Keene, and taken to the colonies where our other uncle, Sir Gaston Keene, had already immigrated.

"Bradford inherited Lord John's estate, only to lose it to the colonial rebels in the recent revolution. I'm ashamed to say Uncle Gaston fell in league with the rebels, but that meant his estate was safe. When Gaston's daughter, Abigail, died, his grandson, my cousin Gregory, should have inherited Gaston's estate at Gaston's death. However, because Gregory remained loyal to the Crown, as had my brother, the demented old man disinherited him and left the bulk of his estate, including the Keene family jewels, to some strange young American girl and her half-breed fiancé."

Crane still could not understand Canfield's point and how he was to be involved.

"I can see you still don't fully understand," Canfield chuckled. "No matter, that's all you need to know for now. That, and the fact I'm the only living blood relative of Bradford Keene, and therefore should rightfully inherit his estate, which now includes Uncle Gaston's estate.

"You see, Crane, I don't intend to stand by and let a fortune in jewels—that should rightfully be mine—slip away to some common colonial woman."

The guest nervously noted the cold, determined glare in his host's eyes and pitied anyone who stood in the man's way.

"Tell me, Crane, what would you say to a share in a jewel collection valued at well over three hundred thousand pounds?"

This sudden development caught the actor by surprise. He stared at his host in stunned silence as Canfield added, "All you need to do is assist me in a little charade."

1

It was a cool cloudy day in September. Red and yellow splashes of maple, ash, and hickory leaves brightened the otherwise gloomy atmosphere of the day.

Andrew Macklin was in his silversmith shop at the front of the house, working with the tools inherited from his father. It had been nearly a year since Cornwallis surrendered at Yorktown, that historic day in September 1781, and the treaty officially ending the Revolutionary War was still being negotiated in Paris. Mac had been honorably discharged with a personal letter of commendation from General Washington. With the war behind him, he and his new bride, Jessica, had settled comfortably into their Dunston, Virginia, home.

Jessica was in the kitchen taking advantage of the coolness of the day to do her baking. With her face flushed from the heat of the fire, she brushed back a tendril of her dark chestnut brown hair that had escaped the ribbon at the nape of her neck. Then she smiled with satisfaction and peered into the tin box oven just inside the large fireplace to savor the sweet aroma of the fresh bread.

Down the hall toward the front of the house, Jess heard the door of the shop open. In a moment, Mac's tall muscular build filled the low doorway of the kitchen as she looked up from the hot loaves of bread she was just turning out onto the table. His rugged features with deep brown eyes, very dark hair, and ruddy complexion had set Jessica's heart aflutter from the first moment she saw him. That effect had not diminished over the past two years since their first meeting.

Mac took a deep breath of the aroma of freshly baked bread. "Four, good. I'm starved!" he declared as he admired the golden brown loaves.

She smiled. "I baked an extra one in case Franklin arrives tonight. The other two are for the Newtons. Mrs. Newton's down with the grippe. If you'll wash up, I'll have a bite of lunch ready in a minute, then I'll take these over to Mrs. Newton."

Mac reached over to pinch off a small piece from one of the loaves.

"Not that one!" Jessica warned quickly. "That's the prettiest one."

"What?" her husband grinned. "They're all the same."

"No," she replied seriously. "This one's for us; it's a little lopsided. The best one must be saved for Franklin."

"I doubt Franklin will measure to see if it's perfectly shaped before he eats any of it," Mac chuckled.

Jess sighed. "I just want everything to be perfect. He's your best friend, and I don't want him to think you've married someone who can't make a proper home for you. I even used his mother's recipe for the molasses cookies. They're not quite the same, though. Maybe I shouldn't serve them."

Mac studied her a moment. Considering the dangerous adventures they had survived together and the level-headed courage he'd seen her display in the face of crises, it seemed almost comical that she should be so concerned about cookies and loaves of bread and making a good impression on his friend. When she looked up at Mac with those big gray-green eyes filled with adoration, his heart was overwhelmed again by the reality of his love for her, and he gently took her hand and drew her into a warm embrace.

"Jess," he smiled, the light in his dark eyes dancing with joy. "Franklin already envies me for marrying the prettiest girl in the whole country."

Dr. Franklin Barton urged his black horse into a quicker pace as he was anxious to end his journey. It had been a long ride from Barleyville, South Carolina, to the Virginia hamlet of Dunston. Although a young man in his twenties, his gaunt appearance, wearily slumped shoulders, and empty left sleeve were lasting reminders of the Battle of Camden where he had nearly died two years before. Had it not been for his old friend, Andrew Macklin, finding him in time after the battle, he would have lost more than just his left arm in that dismal colonial defeat.

Now, the doctor was on his way to visit his old friend, Macklin, and was eager to see him again. He was also slightly curious to see how his chum was settling into his new roles of husband and civilian silversmith.

By midafternoon, the young doctor was riding into Dunston, a pleasant village nestled at the foot of the mid-section of the Appalachian Mountains. He had no difficulty finding the two-story, white frame house with the directions he'd been given, and soon he was standing on the front porch waiting for his knock to be answered. When the door swung open, he grinned and announced,

"Well, I see you're surviving the little bride's cooking so far."

"Franklin!" Mac greeted his friend enthusiastically. "Come in, come in. We were wondering if you'd arrive today. Jess'll be back shortly. One of the neighbors down the lane has been ill and she's looking in on her."

Franklin noted that Mac seemed to be thriving in his new lifestyle. He was the picture of robust health and good humor. Friends since the age of five, Franklin had watched Mac endure the loss of his mother and younger brother to smallpox and his father less than a year later to a broken heart. The first year of the war had taken Mac's remaining brother, Roger, who had been killed at Savannah. Mac tended to be rather serious by nature, and the tragic losses he'd suffered along with the difficult struggles of the war had intensified his stony demeanor. Franklin was pleased to see a new light in his friend's eyes and the grim set of his jaw now relaxed.

Mac showed him the silversmith shop and the work he and Jessica's brother, Robbie McClaren, had been doing to renovate the old house. After the tour, they settled on the porch with some lemonade and the molasses cookies Jessica had made.

"They don't taste quite the same as your mother's," Mac grinned, "but she's getting there."

Franklin finished his last chewy morsel. "I must say, married life seems to agree with you, Mac. It's been a long time since I remember seeing you smile so much."

"I highly recommend it," the newlywed declared as he leaned back in his chair and stretched comfortably.

Franklin went on. "Granted, I can understand why any man would turn himself inside out for someone as lovely as Jessica, but I've been curious how a confirmed lone wolf like yourself adapts to being involved so closely with someone."

"Sometimes I wonder that, too," Mac replied. "For some strange reason I find myself telling her things I've never shared with anyone. Even stranger than that, she really is interested when I do. Oh, we have our differences. I mean, she's normally reasonable and sweet tempered, but she can get something in her head and can be as determined—no, just plain stubborn—as any army mule you ever saw! Of course, if she weren't, she'd have never convinced me to help her make that journey to Charleston, and we might have gone our separate ways."

"Ahh, that's it then," Franklin interjected. "You're two of a kind."

The man gave a wry smile in protest, then his grin softened. "I guess all newlyweds have a few adjustments to make. Maybe ours just seem a little easier than most because of those awful long periods during the war when we were apart.

"If we disagree on something, I guess we're a little more careful in considering each other's feelings because we remember what it was like to be away from each other. And when she looks up at me with those big, beautiful eyes, all I can think of is how terribly empty my life was without her."

"You do have it bad, don't you?" Franklin observed with a droll smile.

As they fell silent, Mac reflected on how he and Jessica had first met during the war. While on one of his missions, he had been wounded and was trying to evade the British patrols searching for him. Jessica and her father had been on their way to deliver two thoroughbred horses to Charleston, South Carolina, when they encountered him and ended up saving his life.

Mac's attention was drawn back to his friend. Franklin sighed, "Don't you miss the excitement of those days back in Lexington just before the war when you were working out your silversmith apprenticeship with your great-uncle?"

"And you were going to medical college in Boston to follow in your father's footsteps," Mac added.

"Yes," Franklin chuckled. "We were a couple of wide-eyed lads used to life in a small village, suddenly caught up in the midst of the excitement, listening to Mr. Revere and Old Sam Adams during those meetings of the Sons of Liberty. I'll never forget the stirring I felt just imagining what a tremendous task we were taking on.

"Do you remember that night shortly after the skirmishes at Lexington and Concord when a bunch of us were sitting around wondering what might happen next? Someone was mumbling over in the corner about the foolishness of biting off more than one can chew. You stood up, broke that stony silence of yours, then proceeded to remind us of the rightness and necessity of shedding our very life's blood, if necessary, to create a new independent nation of free men—men who would, hopefully, handle liberty in such a responsible way that it'd work for the well-being of the nation's people as a whole."

Mac felt somewhat embarrassed. "Those are your words. I'm sure I was nowhere near that eloquent."

"Yes, you were. I told myself right then and there that your talents were being wasted in a silversmith shop. You should have been rubbing elbows with Ben Franklin and Tom Jefferson, right up there in the Continental Congress helping direct the way this new government is going."

"Whoa—wait a minute," Mac cautioned. "I think that's the only time I ever had the nerve to get up and say any such thing, and I was sorry afterwards for making such a spectacle of myself. You were always the one who had a way with words."

"That's probably true." Franklin tugged at his lapel with a statesmanlike air. "I guess you were more valuable as an agent and courier," he mused. "After you'd spent so much time with your grandparents at the Cherokee mission at Iron Mountain and learned to speak Delaware, Cherokee, and French and mimic your grandfather's Scottish brogue, it's no wonder Washington commended you for moving as easily in the city as on a wilderness trail."

Mac nodded in casual acceptance of the compliment, which referred to the letter of thanks written by General Washington he'd received when he'd been honorably discharged after being seriously wounded.

Franklin lifted his empty sleeve. "I guess the one thing that's helped me adjust to this and having to give up practicing medicine has been the opportunity to become involved with politics. I'd never let on to Father, but I was never as comfortable being a doctor as he is. You know how I've always had a keener interest in law and government. I'm really much happier as a representative to the South Carolina Assembly than I ever was patching up broken bones and bleeding people with those slimy leeches."

Franklin paused and looked squarely at Mac. "You ought to consider running for office yourself, Mac. The treaty hasn't been signed with England yet, but it's only a matter of time. Then the real work will begin in trying to make this grand experiment a success. We'll be needing men like you who've been in the middle of the fight and remember what it was like. The House here in Virginia will soon be choosing new representatives. With the endorsement you could get from Washington, and even

Jefferson, you'd have no trouble at all winning a seat. What do you say?"

Mac studied him a moment, then shook his head. "I say things are in very good hands with folks like you and Tom Jefferson and General Washington. Besides, here comes the best reason of all for me to stay put and concentrate on a simple, quiet life."

Franklin followed Mac's gaze toward the gate to see a slender young woman with dark chestnut brown hair hurrying toward them. The radiant glow of her face and the quick spring to her step as she hurried to greet them made it obvious that she was perfectly happy right where she was, too.

Seeing the smile on Jessica's face when she spotted Mac, Franklin wondered what it would be like to be regarded with such obvious adoration. He decided that being the object of such affection would be reason enough for any man to find some cozy little corner in which to settle down.

Knowing that Jessica and Mac had experienced several dangerous adventures together, Franklin was glad that his friends had found a tranquil life in this sleepy little Virginia village. He prayed that it would continue that way for years to come. Little did he realize that the tranquility would last only one more week.

2

Charleston Harbor at last! Over a week later than promised by the captain, but the month-long voyage was behind him now. Samuel Hampton had begun to think his young life of twenty-two years would end prostrate on the pitching deck of an America-bound sailing vessel. It had been an absolutely horrendous voyage and although Uncle Albert, senior curator of the Cheltenham Museum, had repeatedly assured him of the importance of this assignment, Samuel had seriously begun to wonder whether his uncle was really trying to get rid of him. He would much rather have been at home enjoying the comfort and civility of his scholastic pursuits at the university. If the ship voyage had been insufferable, what could he expect from a wilderness country filled with wild Indians and rebellious renegades from England and the Continent.

The young man groaned, wondering if he would ever see the gently rolling hills of his native England again. As their ship drew closer to its moorings, Hampton began to doubt the wisdom of having accepted his uncle's offer.

After all, what good would a large commission and the position of junior board member on the museum board be if he didn't survive to collect them!

The trip had not been made any more pleasant by his companion, George Melden, a professional security agent. From the very start Melden had made it clear that his job would only be hampered by having to mollycoddle his client's nephew. Melden felt that this was especially true for him during the post-war turmoil. After recently winning her independence from England, the new United States of America in 1782 was not the best place for an Englishman. The official peace treaty had not even been signed yet. For that reason, they had chosen to sail on a French West Indies merchant ship from LeHavre, France, instead of Bristol, England.

Late summer squalls had plagued their progress from the very beginning, delaying their arrival along the American shore until September. Standing at the rail, Hampton cast an uncertain eye toward the city beyond the wharves. Until a year ago, when Cornwallis had surrendered at Yorktown, this port had been occupied by British forces. What he wouldn't give to see a good number of red-coat uniforms right now.

The young man gripped the rail to stop his hands from shaking and tried to concentrate on the long letter Uncle Albert had received from the American barrister, Harold Smythe. Wanting to be fully prepared for what he might be facing, he had borrowed the letter from his uncle and studied it so closely he almost knew it by heart.

It told an amazing story of a young American girl who had inherited the Keene family's ancestral jewels. The Keene name was well known in Samuel's home of Cheltenham, England. The story of the brothers, Sir Gaston

22

and Lord John, was still discussed by the old gentlemen of the club.

An extremely bright and ambitious fellow, Sir Gaston Keene had managed to make a grand success of the family shipbuilding enterprise. Discontent with the staid existence of life in the English manor, Gaston had traveled to the colonies as a fairly young man. Immediately captivated by the challenge of American colonial life in South Carolina, he set about building a large estate. In the early days he had supported it largely from wise investments in fur trading and shipping. Later he became interested in raising thoroughbred horses as a hobby.

His brother, Lord John Keene, had served as an officer in His Majesty's Cavalry, campaigning in India. After his return to England, Sir Gaston's glowing letters had convinced him about the potential greatness of his brother's newly adopted home. Lord John had moved to South Carolina to establish a large thoroughbred horse farm of his own. A Scotsman by the name of Rob McClaren, who had served under him as a sergeant in his Dragoons, accompanied Lord John to become stable master of his horses.

McClaren and his wife, Cara, had one son, Robbie Jr., and a daughter, Jessica, born three years after their arrival in the colonies. Over the years, the McClarens and the Keenes had become very close friends.

This fact seemed most curious to Hampton, and only after discussing the matter with a professor of cultural social studies did he begin to grasp the idea. According to Old Professor Wilding, the frontier experience was a leveler of social strata. During the struggle to build in the new land, the two families had developed a camaraderie that would have been impossible between titled landowner and employee in England.

Sir Gaston had taken a special interest in the McClaren children, seeing to it that they had excellent tutors and inviting them often to visit his estate at the South Carolina village of Ellensgate. It appeared that Jessica reminded him of his own daughter, Abigail, who had married an Austrian count. Abigail had passed away leaving a son named Gregory, who lived with Sir Gaston.

According to Smythe's letter, Sir Gaston had disinherited this grandson in favor of the McClaren girl because of some treachery on the grandson's part during the war. To Hampton, Miss McClaren was a peculiar young woman because she had amazingly decided to endow the Cheltenham Museum with the entire Keene jewel collection, valued at well over three hundred thousand pounds. According to Smythe, she felt that the collection should be returned to its ancestral home where its history could be better preserved and it could serve as a memorial to Sir Gaston and Lord John.

The jewels themselves had been secured in a bank in Vienna from the time Lord John had left England. They would remain there until Hampton and Melden returned with the proper documents transferring ownership to the museum. These documents must be signed by Miss McClaren before the process could be completed. Hampton's uncle had assured him that such a generous endowment demanded special care, but he was still not quite clear on the reason it was necessary to acquire her signature in person rather than through the postal system.

Uncle Albert also felt there was a certain amount of urgency to their journey, as Smythe had informed them that Miss McClaren was about to wed. That, in itself, was not so astonishing as the fact that her husband-to-be was half Scot and half Delaware Indian. For all Uncle Albert

24

knew, the two might already be married, and if anything happened to her before his nephew and Melden could secure her signature, Hampton's uncle could only guess whether such a man would honor his wife's wishes.

Then, of course, there was Howard Canfield. Hampton had tried, with little success, to dismiss thoughts of the unpleasant man. It was probably mere coincidence that he had disappeared shortly after the arrival of Harold Smythe's letter. After all, how could he possibly have learned about its contents? His claim to being next in line to inherit the Keene estate was shaky at best, but Hampton knew that Canfield was a devious and determined person.

Wondering if Canfield's sudden departure had been a major reason Uncle Albert felt this journey was necessary, Hampton tried to shrug off his disconcerting thoughts. Considering all he knew about Howard Canfield, Samuel Hampton felt somewhat glad to be accompanied by George Melden, who looked to be well able to handle any difficult situation.

At that moment, he was startled by a hard clap on his shoulder. The burly, six-foot security agent towered over Hampton who was slight of build, standing only five-foot nine.

"Well, there it is, finally," Melden grumbled. "Keep your wits about you, boy, and let me do the talking or we might run into some trouble."

Hampton swallowed hard and nodded. What had he let himself in for, he wondered.

3

A week after Franklin's visit, Jessica was out in the small barn beside the house grooming her horse, Lady Heather Star. The cloudy weather had cleared to a sunny autumn day and she'd talked Mac into taking a break from the shop for a while to ride. Ettinsmoor, Mac's stallion, made a low whuffling noise from his stall as if to remind Jess that he was ready for some exercise, too.

With a final stroke of the brush along Lady's satiny coat, Jess turned toward the other stall. "Patience, fella. Mac will be here in a moment, and we'll all get a little exercise this afternoon. He must have gotten sidetracked. I'll go see what's keeping him."

She patted Lady lovingly then walked out of the barn toward the house. Jess could see her husband standing on the porch looking at a piece of paper. Drawing closer, she could tell by the expression on his face and the look in his dark eyes that he was upset by something.

Apprehensively, she hurried up the steps. "What is it, Mac?"

He didn't answer.

"Mac?"

"It's a letter from Grandmother Macklin," he said finally. "Grandfather's not well, and there's a problem."

"What's wrong?" Jess glanced over his arm toward the letter and was a little surprised when he folded it before she could read anything.

"It's the mission," he answered with a grim sigh. "Some land company's wanting to buy the settlement land and all of the buildings at the mission for a town site."

"Why? Isn't there enough other land in the valley they could take? Why the settlement?" The deeply furrowed brow and angry set of Mac's jaw disturbed her. She hadn't seen him so perturbed since that terrible time a year and a half ago when Bradford Keene had threatened their lives.

"The land's cleared, the water wells are already dug, and the soil's about the most fertile in the area. But the biggest reason is it's Indian mission land." The bitterness in his voice surprised her.

Jess realized that during his life Mac had experienced a few instances of prejudice because he was part Indian, but he had never been this upset before. Seeing this sudden bitterness in him was strangely unsettling to her.

"I have to go to Iron Mountain, Jess, and see what's going on."

"Of course," she agreed, running a quick mental checklist of things she must do to get ready for the three-and-a-half-day journey. "I'll pack our things quickly and we can leave first thing in the morning."

"I'll be going alone," her husband replied. "And I'll leave this afternoon." With that, he abruptly turned and went into the house, leaving her standing alone smarting from his uncharacteristically brusque manner.

Mac walked into his shop. He hadn't meant to snap at Jess, and he knew he would apologize as soon as he returned from delivering the pewter water pitcher he had just finished. The anger boiling inside had kept him from telling Jessica all the news in the letter. It was too infuriating to even talk about and there was no need to upset her with the tragic story of the cruel and senseless attack on the Christian Delaware Indians in Pennsylvania. The additional news of the threat to his grandparents' mission and his Cherokee friends at Iron Mountain only compounded his inner turmoil. As much as he hated being away from Jess for even a day, he could not allow her to accompany him. The Pennsylvania incident was tragic proof that the possibility of a conflict between White settlers and the Indians was no place for innocent bystanders. Wanting time to cool down, he left to deliver the pitcher without saying anything to Jessica.

When he returned Jess was sitting and waiting, dressed in a Brunswick riding habit of hunter green, her wide-brimmed hat placed jauntily upon her head. On the floor beside her chair was a leather valise, a small reed basket, and two leather saddlebags packed for the trail.

"What's this?" Mac asked as he entered the drawing room. "I said I'd go alone, Jess. I want to get there as quickly as possible. I have a very bad feeling about this."

Puzzled by the unusual irritability in his voice, Jess replied, "Lady and I will keep up. Please, Mac. I can be of help to your grandparents. I'd love to visit with them both."

"No. You haven't been feeling well, and the trip won't be easy. You need to stay here." He went to the small writing desk. "I'll drop off this note to the Carters to let them know there'll be a slight delay in delivering their order of wine goblets."

Watching him closely, Jess became more perplexed by this uncharacteristically stubborn attitude, yet she realized he was not upset with her personally. "I've just been a little tired, that's all," she calmly replied. "You know I can manage on the trail."

"No!" Mac slammed his pen down impatiently and stood to face her. "I'm going alone and that's final."

Never before had he been so abrupt with her, and it frightened her a little. She didn't fear Mac, but she did fear that the situation must be more serious than he was indicating. Jess stood up.

"Mac, please. We can make camp tonight on Stony Creek, and I'll cook you the best fresh fish dinner you've had since we were on the trail to Charleston." Placing her hand on his arm, she looked up at him with pleading eyes.

Studying her for a long moment, he suddenly felt as uneasy about leaving her behind as taking her along. Finally, he sighed, "Robbie warned me this stubborn streak of yours might someday be a disadvantage." A slight smile appeared, momentarily softening the grim set of his jaw and making Jessica feel a little better.

His reference to her older brother, Robbie, also helped. Mac and Robbie were good friends and had worked together during the war. After their life and death struggle with Bradford Keene, a strong bond had developed between the three of them. Even now that bond continued to grow. The newlyweds had chosen the little town of Dunston because it was only a few miles from Cherry Hills Farms, the horse farm now owned by Jessica's parents and operated by her father and Robbie. Her older brother's many visits with them were always happy occasions.

That night camping on the Virginia banks of Stony Creek, the couple enjoyed a fish dinner that was as delicious as the first time Jess had cooked one for Mac two and a half years earlier on their way to Charleston. Mac apologized for being so short with her, but his mood remained grim. He seemed so preoccupied that Jess had little success in keeping any conversation going. Finally she decided to turn in, hoping he would feel better in the morning.

Mac helped her spread a blanket on the ground and fold the saddle blankets into pillows. Jess settled on the blanket and unfolded a second blanket they could use for cover. A contemplative Mac added another piece of wood to the fire.

"Aren't you coming to bed?" she asked.

"Not just yet," he replied. "I think I'll sit up a while, keep the fire going. Get some sleep, Jess. We'll be covering a lot of miles tomorrow."

The young wife lay down and pulled the blanket over herself, too tired to think about tomorrow. Just before drifting off to sleep, she watched her husband gazing into the darkness surrounding their campsite. She was reminded of the first night of their journey to Charleston when he had agreed to help her take Lady and Ettinsmoor to the port because Bradford had sold them. Mac had been a stranger to her then, but she had trusted him to help her after her father had been seriously injured and forced to remain with Franklin's father, the senior Dr. Barton, in Barleyville. Somehow, she had felt an inexplicable confidence in him, a confidence that had been justified through one trial after another.

Just as she had been glad he had given in and decided to help her get to Charleston, she was glad he had allowed her to come on this journey. From the very first, they had worked as a team meeting each difficulty together. She wasn't about to sit idly by twiddling her thumbs if she could help Mac in any way. This time she was filled with a strange foreboding. Somehow, she couldn't help feeling that the past five months of peaceful happiness they had enjoyed had been merely the calm before a gathering storm.

When the fire had died down a bit, Mac added another log. While up, he went over to check on Lady and Ettinsmoor, picketed close by. Ettinsmoor gave a low grumbly sound as Mac stopped to give him a scratch behind his ears and along the middle of his forehead.

"You two get some rest. We have a long way to go tomorrow," he spoke quietly. The big stallion gave his master a slight nudge to encourage more scratching, and Mac obliged. Standing there with the horses, he too was reminded of that trip to Charleston when he had first encountered Jess, her father, and these two remarkable thoroughbreds.

It had been a difficult journey in so many ways, yet Mac cherished the memory of it as much as Jessica did, for his entire life had been changed by it. Although the purpose of the journey had been to deliver the two horses to be shipped to the West Indies, circumstances resulted in the horses being returned to Sir Gaston's estate and ultimately willed to Jessica and Mac when Sir Gaston died. He and Jessica treasured these two animals.

Leaning back against a tree trunk, he glanced over at Jess. As she slept, he remembered those nights on the trail when he would sit up keeping watch. The apprehension knotted inside then had been caused by the realization of the danger she was in, traveling with an American agent right under the noses of the British troops occupying the colony of South Carolina. He had the same feeling now, but this one was due to not knowing what they would face when they reached the mission.

Sighing deeply, Mac wondered why in the world he had given in to Jess. It was foolish to have allowed her to come. Although little comfort, he knew that if worse came to worst and it became necessary to move his grandparents away from the mission, Jess could be very helpful in convincing the elder Macklins to go, and knowing his grandparents, this would not be an easy task.

Early the next morning after a quick breakfast of ham and pan bread, the couple broke camp and started out again just as the first warming rays of sun began touching the treetops with golden light. They rode at a steady pace all day, stopping at brief intervals to rest the horses, then pressing on. When they stopped that evening to make camp, Jess was exhausted but refused to admit it. Although their pace had been steady, she knew Mac had not pushed as hard as he would have if he had been alone.

They ate their dinner silently. She was too tired to chat and he was still preoccupied. Jess fell asleep shortly after the meal, and Mac kept watch again late into the night. When he did nod off, it was only for short periods of light dozing.

The second full day passed as the first. Mid-morning they splashed across a shallow ford of the Catawba River. Continuing south through low rolling hills cloaked in the blaze of autumn, they pressed the pace. By pushing this way and traveling late, they were able to cross into South Carolina the next morning. Their trail turned more westerly and began climbing into the mountains. As the trail steepened, their pace slowed. By the afternoon of the third day, Mac could see that Jessica was exhausted. Although she insisted they continue on, he decided to make camp early. Originally he had planned to stop a few miles east of the narrow gap giving access to the Chalequah Valley, which would have meant their arrival at the mission would be by noon the next day.

"Mac, this means we won't be at Iron Mountain until late tomorrow afternoon," Jess lamented as Mac dismounted in a small clearing just off the trail. "It really isn't necessary to stop this early."

"We've pushed Lady and Ettinsmoor pretty steadily. They can use the rest as much as we can," Mac replied as he loosened Ettinsmoor's cinch.

Jessica dismounted and patted Lady gently, speaking to her as she loosened the saddle. "It won't be much farther, girl, but Mac's right. You deserve a good rest. Maybe a long afternoon nap would help someone else, too."

Mac gave her a side glance but said nothing as he pulled Ettinsmoor's saddle off. Jess removed Lady's saddle and as the two of them gave their horses a brisk brushing, Jess continued talking.

"You'll love the Chalequah Valley, Lady. It's a very special place, you know. Of course, the spring wildflowers'll be gone and the meadow grass has turned brown, but it's still beautiful. I know you were upset because you had to stay in Virginia with Robbie's horses when Mac and I came up here for the wedding, but you'll get to see it now."

Jess looked over at Mac and thought about that beautiful spring morning five months earlier. The hills around the valley had been appropriately clad in bright spring-blossoming trees and bushes. The entire valley floor was a sea of nodding wildflowers dancing in a gentle fragrant breeze. So many people had come for the wedding that the small meetinghouse could not hold them all, so the ceremony had been held outside.

Grandfather Macklin had proudly presided over the occasion. Standing on the green at the center of the village and shaded by the huge live oak, they had exchanged their vows. Jess had stood before Mac, looking up at him and seeing his love for her shining in his dark brown eyes. Although he was expert at masking his feelings, on that day it was clear that he didn't care if the whole world knew how deeply he cared for her or how happy it made him to see her adoration.

However, the past three days had been different. Mac's mask was firmly in place. In contrast to their wedding day, his face had been set in a stony grimness that worried her. She had tried teasing him into a better mood several times, but each attempt had fallen flat. Jessica was becoming a bit impatient and almost angry with his coolness. The fact that he had not allowed her to read the letter from his grandparents was puzzling. Since their marriage, she had felt as keenly interested in the elder Macklins' well-being as he was. Now she was certain he was hiding something from her. He was shutting her out and it hurt deeply.

"You know, Lady," Jessica began again as she put oats in a feed bag and fastened it to Lady's halter, "James and Marion Macklin—that's Mac's grandparents—they've lived at Iron Mountain for nearly forty years, I think. They came from Scotland, you know. His other grandmother was Delaware Indian. I only got to meet her once, but I remember what a gracious lady she was. Her name was She-wan-ikee. I can't remember exactly how they all got together, but I think it was up in Rhode Island or . . ."

"Pennsylvania," Mac corrected quietly.

"Yes, of course," Jess agreed, still directing her remarks to Lady but smiling to herself for at last getting Mac's attention. "I think Grandfather and Grandmother Macklin first came to the colonies to work with the Delaware Indians in southeastern Pennsylvania. That's when She-wan-ikee and her little girl, Lelia, came to live with them. An epidemic or something . . ."

"Measles," Mac added as he fitted Ettinsmoor's feed bag in place.

"Yes, now I remember," Jess said as she stroked Lady's neck. "Wiped out nearly the whole Lenape village. Lenape—that's what the Delaware were called back then. Anyway, Grandfather and Grandmother Macklin had a son by the name of Andrew, and he and Lelia grew up together. They married and had three little boys. The oldest one was named Andrew Jr. after his father, but everybody called him Mac."

Mac walked over beside her. "I'm sure Lady's fascinated by this history lesson, but do you think we could fix a bite of dinner for ourselves now?"

"Sure." Jess turned toward her horse. "I'll be back to tell you the rest, Lady. I think you'll find the story very interesting about how the mission at Iron Mountain was established, that is if I can get Mac to refresh my memory about it."

Glancing up at him, Jessica was relieved to see a smile broaden on his face. He slipped his arm across his wife's shoulders. As they walked over to set up camp, he sighed, "I'm sorry, Jess. I haven't been very good company, have I!"

She didn't reply. She was just happy to see him finally smile again.

The afternoon shadows were growing long as the two people relaxed beside the fire with a cup of coffee. Finally

Jess said, "I really would like for you to tell me again how your grandparents came to Iron Mountain. I think you've only told me bits and pieces of it. I want to be sure I have it right in case I decide to tell it to Lady some time."

Mac nodded. "Okay. What do you want to hear?"

"Well, what made them decide to leave Pennsylvania and come here?"

"The mission in Pennsylvania was already pretty well established when they arrived." Mac remembered the terrible news in Gran's letter and frowned.

Jessica drew his attention back to her question and with some effort, he concentrated on the story of his grandparents instead of the recent tragedy.

"About five years after they arrived in the colonies, Grandfather made a trip south to visit a friend who had just come over from Scotland. On his way back, he came across a small band of Cherokee whose village had been nearly wiped out by a smallpox epidemic. Only a few families survived. Grandfather stayed with them to help the survivors recover.

"Quiet Bear's father was the only surviving tribal elder, and he became quite a challenge to Grandfather. Pretty crafty old fella, apparently. Somehow he convinced Grandfather that if everything Grandfather had been telling them about God's mercy was true, surely someone would come to his people to help them and teach them. The mission there was well established, as I said, and the pastor in charge had things well under control so, of course, it didn't take long for Grandfather to feel like he was the one being called to help Quiet Bear's band.

"My grandmother, She-wan-ikee, and Gran Macklin became as close as sisters, so she and my mother came with them when Grandfather moved everyone south.

Four other families from a nearby village that had suffered a similar plight joined them, and they moved as one group to Iron Mountain. For the past forty years they've lived a quiet life, sheltered from conflict with settlers and the war."

Mac grew quiet as he pictured the beautiful Chalequah Valley nestled high in the southern tip of the Appalachian mountains in western South Carolina. The Cherokee called this country of gently rounded, tree-lined slopes the "Shaconage," the place of the blue smoke, because of the hazy mists that settled over the mountain range like a smoky shroud.

Although his parents, Lelia and Andrew Sr., eventually settled in Barleyville, South Carolina, Mac had spent nearly every summer of his childhood at Iron Mountain. After his parents died, he and his younger brother, Roger, moved in with their grandparents. The Iron Mountain village represented an important part of Mac's life.

He had explored the surrounding slopes with their rocky, brush-choked gorges where wild rivers careened down granite chutes. His playground had been forests that teemed with wildlife—black bear, mountain lion, lynx, bobcat, raccoon, deer, possum, squirrels, foxes, and rabbits. The boy had often been enthralled by the sight of majestic eagles soaring along the mountain ridges, and he had frequently wakened to the songs of larks and thrushes. The trees and sky were alive with a myriad of different birds, from wild turkeys, eagles, and hawks to tiny ruby-throated hummingbirds and bright black and yellow orioles. To think of the pristine beauty of the valley being taken over by some land-hungry speculators was a weight almost too heavy for his heart.

Jess realized her husband's thoughts were wandering again. Determined not to allow this to happen, she quickly asked, "Mac, do you think we'll have time to ride up to our honeymoon cabin?"

It took a moment for her words to register. "We'll see," he finally answered.

Their honeymoon cabin was actually an old hunter's cabin at the north end of the valley that had been built several years before the Macklins and Cherokee had arrived. Jess and Mac had spent a week at the cabin after their wedding.

With nightfall, Jessica went to sleep early and Mac sat beside the fire, looking out into the darkness. For a while he had been able to put aside the deep foreboding that weighed heavily upon him, but now it loomed about him more oppressively than ever. Haunting images of his Lenape ancestors seemed to dance before him in the illusive shadows cast by the flickering firelight. The slow, rhythmic beat of the bull-hide drum echoed along with his pulse, and he could almost hear the chanting song of the tribal singer. It was a song from the heart of a people who believed no man could own the land any more than one could hold title to the air. This song had been drowned out by the hungry cry of those Europeans escaping the poverty and oppression of a culture where the measure of a man seemed to be the amount of land he could possess and subdue. Mac had long felt that this valley was beyond the reach of that conflict. Now, he was not so sure.

4

As Jessica had predicted, she and Mac finally arrived at the mission late in the afternoon of the fourth day of travel. After leaving Lady and Ettinsmoor at the settlement stable, they climbed the short slope to the Macklins' cabin in silence. Jess stood beside her husband on the porch of the log house and waited for their knock to be answered. She took a deep breath of freshly scented autumn air, relieved the long journey was over.

The view out across the valley was breathtaking in the late afternoon light. A sun-washed haze hung in a gossamer mist over the mountains to the west. The warm fall colors of the thickly forested hillsides deepened to an indigo blue that would soon be black in shadow. Scattered puffy banks of clouds trailed across the sky just above the horizon taking on a golden fringe of light as the last slanting rays of sunlight shot across the western sky.

The door was opened by a small, slender woman with snow-white hair secured in a neat bun at the back of her head. Mac's grandmother was delighted to see them standing there.

With tears brimming in her bright blue eyes, she hugged her grandson with almost desperate relief and turned to Jess. "Jessica, my dear, I'm so glad you came, too," she said, hugging Jess tightly.

"How's Grandfather?" Mac asked as they walked inside.

"He'll feel much better now that you're here, Mac, dear. Come, I'll take you to him."

The cabin was solidly built of hand-hewn logs notched at the corners to rest snugly one on top of the other. The mud and straw mixture filling in the chinks had long since hardened to keep out any drafts. The windows were equipped with outside shutters for protection against the wind, snow, and rain. Panes of real glass had been recently installed, a gift from Jess and Mac purchased with some of the inheritance money Jess had received from Sir Gaston's estate.

The cabin was made up of three rooms and a loft. There was one large main room with a smaller room divided off on either end as bedrooms. The focus of the main room was a large fireplace that dominated the wall opposite the door. This was the cooking area as well as a source of heat and light.

A large trestle table stood at one side of the fireplace; a long high-backed deacon's bench stood at the other. A rocking chair and a smaller chair had been placed near the bench.

In one corner of the room a cot of timbers smoothed with a drawknife was attached to the wall along one side and at the head. It had a straw-filled mattress resting on criss-crossed rope supports.

Over the left side of the room was a sleeping loft where Mac and his two brothers had slept during their summer visits. It had later become Mac and Roger's room when the two boys came to live with their grandparents after the death of their parents and youngest brother, Jamie.

Gran led them into a small, cozy bedroom furnished sparsely, but comfortably, with hand-hewn furniture. James Macklin lay in the bed covered by a colorful patchwork quilt. His deeply lined, angular face brightened upon seeing his grandson and Jessica enter.

"The Lord be praised!" Grandfather declared in a thankful whisper. Sitting up slowly, he blinked back tears of joy and reached for Mac's hand as his grandson came to his bedside. "Hello, lad. I knew you'd come."

Mac's heart sank a little, seeing his grandfather's weakened condition. Swallowing the lump in his throat, Mac forced a broad smile and gripped his grandfather's hand tightly.

For a long moment, Grandfather gazed with pride and thanksgiving at his grandson. Continuing to hold Mac's hand, he reached out to Jess. "And who's this lovely vision?" he teased gently as Jess stepped forward. "Jessica, m'dear, how did the lad ever talk you into makin' that long journey?"

Mac and Jess exchanged brief glances. Jess was smiling, but Mac became very sober once more.

Placing a kiss of greeting on Grandfather's weathered cheek, Jessica declared, "How could I ever pass up the chance to visit my two favorite people in the world?"

"The sight of you two is like a tonic for the soul," Grandfather sighed happily as he settled back on his pillow.

"Jessica," Gran said, "you look exhausted, dear. Come, let's leave these two to their chatting and we'll have a cup of coffee."

Jess squeezed Grandfather's hand then followed Grandmother Macklin back into the main room.

The Macklins' cabin was a comfortable, inviting home, and Jessica couldn't imagine Mac's grandparents having to give it up. She sat down at the table and Gran poured the coffee.

"I'm not quite sure what we're going to do, Jessica." Gran shook her head as she sat down across from Jess. "James hasn't been well for some time. About a month ago we were paid a visit by a man named Carlson Frye with the Fair View Land Company. He offered to buy the land here at the mission and throughout the settlement for a rather good price. He seemed quite nice. When James told him we couldn't sell because the families in the settlement would be displaced with nowhere to go, he left, and we thought that would be the end of it.

"Then three weeks ago, he returned with a letter from the South Carolina Assembly saying he was authorized to buy the land at a fair price and that we had to sell to him!"

The look of alarm on Gran's face was disconcerting and Jess tried to reassure her. "Surely they can't force you to sell if you don't want to." She had heard that land speculators had started flocking to the frontier since the war, hoping to make large profits in the western lands. Because it was fairly remote from the new trails opening up to the west, no one had even considered the possibility that someone might try to move in on the mission land.

With a furrowed brow, Gran replied, "Their papers looked very official. That's why I wrote you and Mac. James thinks that with the country in such a depressed state economically and the new government still on such shaky ground, there'll be nothing that can be done on our behalf. I'm afraid this upset will be too much for him."

After a long silent moment, Gran sighed then squared her shoulders. "Enough of that. Thank you for coming, too, Jessica dear. I know it isn't an easy trip, but it's so good to see you. How is everything at home?"

"Just wonderful." Jessica's smile brightened the mood considerably. "I didn't think I could ever be so happy. Mac and Robbie did a marvelous job renovating the old shop and our living quarters, and Mac is really doing well considering the times. Most of his business has been on a barter basis, which has worked out well, but he's gotten some orders from several of the larger planters, too. Oh, Gran, he has done some beautiful work. He's so talented."

The older woman smiled and teased gently, "You don't think much of him, do you, dear?"

Jess grinned sheepishly and said, "Does it show that plainly?"

"If your eyes sparkled any brighter, they'd be flashing fire. You're good for Mac, Jessica. We knew on his first visit after meeting you that you were someone very special. I'd never seen him happier than on your wedding day. He may be my grandson, but he really is an exceptional young man and deserves the best. I believe he's found that in you."

This glowing statement of approval made Jess blush and before she could reply, Gran looked at the pendant watch hanging around her neck and said, "Oh my, it's getting late. We must get some dinner started."

While helping prepare the meal, Jess studied Mac's grandmother carefully. Marion Macklin was a gracious lady with the bearing of an aristocrat but lacking the pretentious air so common among those Jess had known.

Growing up at Cheltenham Farms Jess had become slightly acquainted with some of Lord John's friends. Some were titled gentry and, like Lord John, were very pleasant. However, many others were like his son, Bradford—arrogant and selfish. But Gran was certainly not like Bradford and these men who were totally obsessed with preserving the class structure of the Old World with themselves seated comfortably at the top.

Mac had been talking to his grandfather for nearly an hour when he came out of the bedroom. Still preoccupied with their conversation, he looked up to see Jess setting the dinner plates on the table and said absently, "Jess, Grandfather would like to see you for a minute."

Jess looked quickly toward Gran who nodded with approval.

After Jess left the room, Gran turned to Mac and said, "Mac, dear, please don't be so upset or angry. I've been telling myself that everything is going to be all right. We've been in God's work here for nearly forty years. If it's time for us to move on, well, that's the way it must be; but if the good Lord wants us to keep on working here, no smooth-talking fellow with all of the official papers in the world can move us out. Now that you're here, I'm sure of it."

Mac nodded in agreement, only half-hearing his grandmother's words as he mulled over the situation he had been discussing with his grandfather. He hadn't learned very much more than Gran had first told him in her letter, but it was obvious his grandfather was convinced that the papers presented to them by Carlson Frye had come from the South Carolina Assembly. Mac remembered that Franklin had invited him to come for a visit and see the workings of the state government for himself. That might just be the best way to get to the bottom of this situation.

"Gran, I think I'll ride over to Camden and check on this Fair View Land Company. It shouldn't take more than a day over and the same back. I'll leave first thing in the morning. That should give you and Jess plenty of visiting time and she can rest a bit."

"She does look exhausted, poor dear. I hope the trip wasn't too hard on her, but I'm so glad she came with you. She's such a dear."

"I wasn't so sure it was a good idea after the news about the mission in Pennsylvania, and I didn't know what the situation here would be, but she insisted. When she sets her mind to something . . ." Mac didn't continue.

"You look exhausted, too," Gran patted his arm. "Must you go to Camden in the morning? Can't you rest at least a day first?"

"I'm fine," he reassured her with a smile.

Mac's grandfather was sitting up in bed reading from his well-worn Bible. He was pale, but he smiled broadly when Jessica entered the room.

"Come here, m'child. Sit down."

She sat in the small chair beside his bed and he took her hand.

"Ahhh, little Jessica." His thick Scot's burr reminded her of her father and she felt a slight twinge of homesickness. "I'm so thankful you've come, lass. My dear Marion could use some cheerin' up. How's that grandson of mine treating 'is new bride?"

"He's wonderful, Grandfather Macklin. A bit on the stubborn side, but he certainly inherited his grandfather's charm," she replied graciously.

The old man's blue eyes twinkled with merriment in response to her comment then sobered. "I take it young Andrew wasn't especially encouraging about you comin' along this time."

Jess tried to dismiss his assumption.

"Be patient with 'im, lass. He's a pretty even-tempered lad until someone begins causin' trouble for 'is family. If my guess is right, he'd rather you not see him lose his temper, nor be around if there's trouble."

"I know you're right, Grandfather. Perhaps I shouldn't have insisted on coming, but I wanted to see you and Gran, and—" She glanced away to avoid his inquisitive gaze.

"And you thought he'd be less likely to do something rash if you were here."

She looked at him in surprise then smiled sheepishly and nodded.

"That's alright, darlin'. There's been more'n one wise little wife who's kept her husband from goin' off half-cocked 'til cooler heads could prevail. I think you were right to come." He patted her hand reassuringly. "Is that Mama's venison stew I smell? I'm gettin' a bit hungry, lass. D'ya suppose you could fetch me a bite to eat?"

"Of course," she answered happily and left to get his dinner.

Stepping out of the bedroom, she noticed Mac was absent.

"He's gone to see Quiet Bear," Gran told her. "He said not to wait dinner on him. I'll just take this tray in to James and you sit down. I'll be back in a moment."

Jess looked out through the window that framed the neat little village stretching down toward the valley. Darkness had fallen, and she could see the faint glow of tiny lamps in cabin windows dotting the settlement streets.

Her thoughts turned to Quiet Bear. The Cherokee Council elder had been blood brother to Mac's father and was now Mac's adopted uncle. Jess remembered Little Sparrow as well, Quiet Bear's niece and the young Cherokee woman who had hoped to be Mac's wife. This last thought made Jess even more glad that she had come along.

Mac returned very late that night. Gran had left a small lantern aglow on the table for him. Jess was lying in bed, half-asleep, in the room that had once been She-wan-ikee's. Mac's Delaware grandmother had lived with the Macklins ever since coming to them in southeastern Pennsylvania. Unfortunately, she had passed away the previous winter before being able to see her grandson marry. The one time she had met She-wan-ikee, Jess had been impressed by her gentility and grace.

"Did you have any supper?" Jess asked in a whisper, watching Mac's shadow as he got ready for bed.

"Did I wake you? I'm sorry. Yes, I had a bite to eat with Quiet Bear." His whispered response came as he sat on the bed to pull off his boots.

Mac climbed into bed and Jess was happy to have his warmth so near. "Could Quiet Bear tell you anything?" she asked.

He sighed deeply. "I wish you hadn't come, Jess. There may be real trouble."

"I'm sorry you feel that way, Mac, but I'm glad I came and so are your grandparents." Lying there in the dark, she could feel the tension mounting between them again.

"I'm riding over to Camden tomorrow to check on this Frye fella and the Fair View Land Company and see why they have so much influence with the Assembly," he told her. "I should be back in two days. Grandfather should be able to travel by that time. You remember meeting Oskati at the wedding?"

"Yes," she answered softly.

"I've asked him to drive the three of you back to Dunston until this thing is settled."

"Do you really think you can persuade your grandparents to leave?" she asked.

"I'm counting on you to help me convince them," his voice came in a deep whisper.

"I'm not sure I can or even should," she replied.

"Why not?" There was that edge in his voice again.

"Well, for one thing, I'm afraid the trip would be too difficult for Grandfather and for another, I'm not sure they should leave." Her own voice had taken on an edge. She waited a moment for him to respond. When he remained silent, she continued, "Grandfather said unless cool heads prevail there could be some rash decisions made. If we stay, there may be less chance of a fight."

"Are you calling me a hothead?"

"Of course not, Mac. It's just . . . I've never seen you so upset. And Grandfather said you're even tempered until someone threatens your family."

"Seems as though you and Grandfather had quite a discussion about me," he commented irritably.

"Really, Mac," she whispered in exasperation. "I just don't want you jumping into a fight. If we're all here, maybe we can think of a way to avoid that."

"Jess, I've just spent the last six and a half years fighting. I've had more than enough to last me a lifetime. I'm certainly not spoiling for a fight, but if it comes to that, I don't want you or them anywhere around. Do you understand?!"

His last sentence was not a question, it was an order— the first uncompromising order he had ever given her. "Mac—" she protested, her independent spirit rankled at being ordered around like a child.

"That's enough said about it. You have no idea what could happen here. Now get some sleep."

With that he turned on his side facing away from her. She turned away with her back to him. Suddenly the small distance between them seemed immense. Jess wiped away an angry, hurt tear.

5

When she awoke the next morning, Jessica sleepily reached for Mac only to find his pillow empty. She raised up and looked around the silent room. He had left without saying good-bye. Then she noticed a folded piece of paper lying on his pillow. Opening it, she found a note and a bracelet made of braided leather strands with delicate shell beads gracefully woven through the strands.

"My darling Jess," the note read, "I'm sorry. Please forgive my ill temper. I couldn't sleep after our discussion, and I finished this for you. I've been working on it for a while and thought it would make a nice peace offering now. I love you. See you in two days. Love, Mac."

Jess admired his handiwork, her heart filled with joyful relief. She only wished she hadn't been so tired and fallen asleep so soundly. Maybe she would have been able to hear him get out of bed and she could have apologized for her own contrariness. Robbie was right; her strong independent nature could be a disadvantage at times. Perhaps this was just part of the adjustment period that most young couples go through as they learn to merge their lives. Slipping the bracelet on her wrist, she fingered it and lovingly traced the strands woven around the smooth milky-white beads made from small shells.

When Jess heard Gran moving about in the kitchen, she hurriedly dressed in a light woolen skirt of pale gray and the soft pink silk blouse her mother had made her just before the wedding. After brushing her hair and quickly tying it back with a pink ribbon, she came out to find Gran already preparing breakfast.

"Good morning, my dear. You look positively aglow this morning. You must have slept well."

"Good morning, Gran," she smiled, touching her bracelet.

"Mac left at dawn, not wanting to wake you," Gran explained. "He said, 'Quicker gone, quicker back!'"

"I know. He left a note. Look at what he made for me." Jessica held out her wrist to display her gift. "Isn't it lovely?"

"Yes, it is," Gran admired. "It's a forever bracelet, did you know?"

"A forever bracelet?"

"Yes," Gran smiled. "It's braided and woven into an unbroken circle symbolizing the never-ending bond of two lives joined together, just as two of the strands are joined by the knot. The third strand stands for our Father God as he blesses the union, making it stronger, just as a three-strand rope is stronger than a two-strand one."

"How wonderful," Jess sighed. Suddenly she felt dizzy by the overwhelming wave of affection.

"Are you all right, Jessica?" Gran asked, noticing her sudden paleness.

"Yes, yes, I'm fine," she said with an uncertain smile.

"Here, sit down. I'll bring you some breakfast."

Jess protested as Gran hurried to the flat iron skillet sitting on the wire tripod just inside the fireplace. She placed a plate of eggs and ham on the table in front of Jess.

"Thank you, Gran, but I don't really feel much like eating. Perhaps just a cup of tea."

Gran handed her a cup of tea and sat down across the table. "Jessica, dear, Mac mentioned this morning that you've been a little under the weather lately. Are you okay?"

"Of course. We've just been very busy getting the house set up and all. I'm fine." She smiled over the cup of tea. "Is there anything I can help you with today?" she asked.

Jess wanted to get off the subject. In this time of limited medical knowledge, poor health was a constant specter haunting mankind. Many times the cures involving leeches, bloodletting, and purgatives were almost as bad as the ailments themselves. Jess had refused to think about not being well, and she had purposely not mentioned her dizziness to Mac. She was surprised that he had noticed and now silently wondered if he had allowed her to come partly because of it. Maybe he was unconsciously afraid that if he left her behind, she might become ill just as his mother and little brother had while he and his father and Roger were away that time. It had been a terrible blow for them to find that smallpox had tragically claimed their lives. Mac had admitted to Jess that he had never really been able to forget that devastating feeling.

Jess was glad Mac had given in to her insistence, for she loved Grandmother and Grandfather Macklin dearly and wanted to help in whatever way she could. Yet, she felt a strange uneasiness about Mac's reaction to their situation. Rereading his note, she tried to reassure herself that she was being silly about this nameless fear haunting her thoughts. Still, it was next to impossible to deny the growing dread that something looming just around the corner would threaten their future happiness together, perhaps even their lives.

Jessica and Gran were just climbing the path to the Macklins' house after a visit with a new mother and baby in the village when Gran stopped short. "Oh dear, he's back."

Jess noticed a light buggy standing in the drive. "Who is it?"

"Carlson Frye," Gran replied grimly. Taking a deep breath, she straightened up a bit and stepped onto the porch.

A rather distinguished looking man greeted them. He was dressed in a dark suit with a flaring split-tail jacket and fine linen stockings as white as the silk ascot tied at the throat of his jacket. By his appearance, Jessica supposed he was a successful businessman. His companion, a taller man than Frye, was dressed in buckskin garb. This man stood back as Frye stepped forward, hat in hand.

"Good afternoon, Mrs. Macklin. It's good to see you again. You've met my business partner, Howard Canfield."

"Mr. Frye. Mr. Canfield," Gran acknowledged warily.

"And who is this lovely young lady?" Frye asked, turning toward Jessica.

"This is our granddaughter-in-law, Mrs. Andrew Macklin. Jessica, this is Mr. Frye and Mr. Canfield."

"How do you do," Jess said politely as she studied the two men.

Carlson Frye had dark hair, graying at the temples, and dark eyes. His smile was pleasant and he seemed genuinely happy to meet Jessica. Canfield stood in the shadows of the porch. She couldn't see his face very clearly but had the impression he was watching them closely. In contrast to his partner's congenial approach, this one seemed sullenly aloof, almost threatening. His presence made her feel much more apprehensive about the Fair View Land Company than she had before.

"As we drove up," Frye was saying, "we saw you walking up from the village. Knowing Mr. Macklin isn't well, we thought it best to wait out here."

"That's very considerate, Mr. Frye. My husband is better but still confined to bed. What, may I ask, brings you here today?" Gran made no move to invite them into the house.

"I wanted to see if you had finally realized the wisdom of accepting our company's offer." Though his words were still quite pleasant, his manner was almost condescending.

"Mr. Frye, you seem to misunderstand the situation here. The only land my husband and I own is this small space we're standing upon. The rest belongs to our people. They've cleared and built and cultivated every square foot. As we told you before, we do not have the right to even consider selling it. As for us, this has been our home for nearly forty years. We still have work to do here."

"Dear Mrs. Macklin," his smile showed fine even teeth, "you and your husband have done a commendable job here. But don't you think it's about time to retire and let these people do for themselves? You deserve a well-earned rest from your labors."

Jessica pulled her shawl about her shoulders. The sun was slipping lower in the western sky casting a pale glow over the valley as an autumn chill settled amidst the lengthening shadows. She seriously doubted that this man was as concerned about Mac's grandparents as he sounded, but she held her tongue.

Gran gently but firmly made one last attempt to indicate their position in the matter. "Mr. Frye, our work here has been a labor of love. It's not the sort of job one retires from. Our people here already do for themselves quite nicely. Our presence here has always been on a basis of their allowing us to stay and operate the school and hold our church services. It's not a matter of us allowing them to stay. They're not children who need watching after. They're human beings in need of discipling in the saving knowledge of our Lord Jesus Christ. That has been, and will continue to be, our job until we're taken home to heaven or sent to another mission field."

Jessica wanted to throw her arms around Gran and hug her. Her gentle eloquence should have convinced anyone that they should look elsewhere for land to buy. However, Canfield and Frye were not just anyone.

Canfield stepped forward. Jess noticed he was a man probably in his fifties. His blue-gray eyes leveled on Gran in an attempt to intimidate her.

"You know, Mrs. Macklin, the way things stand right now, we wouldn't have to offer a farthing for this land. The Indians along the frontier have no legal claim here. The Cherokee signed the Treaty of DeWitts Corner five years ago and gave up all claims to these hills. That leaves this frontier wide open for new settlement. You'd better consider our offer carefully before there's trouble when independents start moving into this valley. Not many of the settlers wanting to move west are as sympathetic to your Indian charges as you."

"Excuse me, Mr. Canfield." Unable to hold her tongue a moment longer, Jessica stepped protectively in front of Gran and declared, "That sounds very much like a threat."

"Not at all, ma'am, just a friendly warning." Canfield smiled, but it was not a friendly smile.

"Perhaps you should pass this friendly warning on to the Iron Mountain Council, since it's their decision to make about their land," Jess added.

Watching Canfield warily, there was something odd about him. She had an eerie feeling that he was not what he appeared to be. Perhaps it was the smooth skin of his face and hands. Jessica found herself wondering uneasily if this man was really a frontiersman.

"Contrary to Mrs. Macklin's statement," Frye once again took the lead, this time addressing Jessica. "These people are very much like children looking to their missionary teachers to advise them. I understand your husband carries quite a bit of influence with one or two of the elders on the Council, Quiet Bear for one. Perhaps we might speak with him. You lovely ladies really shouldn't be bothered with such matters."

Jessica and Gran exchanged perplexed glances and Jess replied, "My husband is away at the moment. He should be back the day after tomorrow. I'm sure he'll be very eager for this to be resolved." She turned to go back into the house with Gran but stopped and said, "By the way, Mr. Frye, just a friendly warning—my husband has several friends in the State Assembly as well as here on the Council. I'm sure he'll get to the bottom of this. It might be a good idea to begin looking elsewhere for your land speculations. Good day, Mr. Frye, Mr. Canfield."

The two men nodded and returned to their buggy.

Once inside, Jessica and Gran remained silent as they listened to the creak and rattle of the wheels over the rocky drive as the two men left.

"I'm sorry, Gran," Jessica finally sighed, still trembling slightly from her agitation. "I didn't mean to meddle, but I'm afraid I just couldn't hold my tongue. It seems they don't want to listen to reason, do they."

Gran gave her a quick hug. "You're right, my dear, they don't. But don't apologize; I appreciate your speaking up."

Jess was concerned by Gran's weary expression. "Why don't you sit down. I'll make some tea."

"Thank you, dear. First I must see about James."

A few minutes later, a firm knock sounded at the door. Standing on the porch was Quiet Bear, a tall, powerfully built man with salt-and-pepper gray hair. The Cherokee elder wore a wide, colorful band of cloth wrapped around his head, a deep blue shirt of homespun, and buckskin trousers. Jess recognized Oskati standing beside him. He was a younger man about Mac's age, who wore a wide cloth band of dark red around his head and buckskin hunting shirt and trousers.

Solemnly, Quiet Bear clasped Jessica's hand. "It is good to see you, Rea' na tani, but I wish you had not come. Things may become very unpleasant here."

"It's good to see you, too, Quiet Bear, and you, Oskati. Please come in and sit down."

"Rea' na tani," Oskati called her by the name the Natiri Indians had given her two years before. The Natiri band belonged to the nation of Iroquois Indians who had allied with the British during the war. They had taken Jess and Mac captive on their way back from Charleston. The name meant "Woman who rides the lightning." (Lightning referred to Lady, Jessica's thoroughbred horse.) She couldn't help feeling a little proud to be addressed this way, for it made her feel that she had truly been accepted by Mac's friends.

"We saw Carlson Frye and Howard Canfield," Quiet Bear began as Jessica poured them a cup of tea. "Are they making more threats?"

"They said if their company's offer isn't accepted, the valley will be taken anyway by independent settlers coming in. He said the Cherokee had signed away this land in a treaty five years ago. Is that true?"

"We signed no treaty. We've not been at war. Why should we sign a treaty?" Quiet Bear declared grimly.

Oskati shook his head sadly. "Whether or not there is a treaty, there will be trouble. Many of our people have been pushed off their land before. They're not willing to let it happen again without a fight."

"Oh dear." They all turned to see Gran Macklin come out of the bedroom. She joined them at the table. "If they fight, what about the women and children?"

"We're getting ready to move them up to High Meadow until the trouble is over," Oskati said. "You must gather what you can and prepare Brother Macklin for the journey. My two cousins have gone ahead to build a shelter for you."

"Bless you, Oskati. Perhaps the move won't be necessary if Andrew is successful in Camden. He's gone to see how much influence Mr. Frye has with the Assembly. He's also going to see what must be done to make certain the claims of the Iron Mountain Cherokee are recognized without dispute."

Jess could see by the silent exchange between the two men that they put little hope in being able to keep their land without a fight . . . a terrible, costly fight.

6

The next day Jessica accompanied Gran down to the meetinghouse in the village. Gran was determined to carry on as usual until something definite was decided. This was the day of the Sewing Circle meeting when all of the ladies of the village were gathering for a morning of sewing, quilting, and visiting.

As they neared the meetinghouse, Jessica spied an older woman talking to a young girl, sitting in the shade of the huge oak tree on the green. She was apparently instructing her on the proper operation of the spinning wheel.

"We didn't realize it at the time," Gran explained with a hint of motherly pride as they watched the two at the spinning wheel, "but my old spinning wheel was one of the most important items we brought along to this valley. The Indians were so bright and eager to learn new things. It wasn't long before James was teaching them how to raise flax and sheep. They were fascinated with being able to turn the flax into linen and the wool into wool thread. Then James showed the men how to build a loom. He's always been a bit of an inventor and so handy with tools he can build almost anything. Although they still rely on deer skins for their clothing, they take great pride in the new fabrics they now make. Their skill is really very impressive."

Clutching Jessica's hand for a moment, Gran seemed suddenly overwhelmed with apprehension. "Jessica, I can't bear the thought of leaving here," she whispered. "These people are our family."

Patting Gran's hand gently, Jessica tried to reassure her. "It's going to be all right. Mac will be able to do something."

As they reached the meetinghouse, Gran took a deep breath and smiled gratefully at Jessica as they entered. Several ladies already inside greeted Gran warmly in Cherokee then acknowledged Jessica in English.

The meetinghouse was a fairly large log structure that served as the place for important gatherings. The Council meetings were held there as well to discuss village business. It also served as a schoolroom during the week and church sanctuary on Sundays.

When the Macklins first came to live among the Cherokee, they did not immediately open a school and church. In the beginning, Mac's father and mother were still young children. Every day Marion Macklin would sit with them under the large live oak tree on the village green. She would read to them from a large family Bible and guide them through lessons in reading, writing, and arithmetic. They each had little wooden paddles with a printed alphabet and pieces of birch bark that they wrote on with charcoal.

The Cherokees' insatiable curiosity and deep desire for learning soon resulted in Lelia and Andrew's friends joining them under the tree each day. Before long several young men approached James to ask if he would teach them these fascinating new skills. Over the years, nearly every one of the village populace, which numbered nearly eighty, had learned to read and write English.

The church had grown the same way only more slowly. For the Macklins, it had been a process of teaching their Christian beliefs during reading lessons in the Bible. Their most effective method of winning confidence and ultimately souls was their kind caring example and courage.

The Macklins were not perfect; however, they had always respected the village leadership and never tried to usurp the Council's authority. Through this approach they had gained the confidence and affection of the entire village.

The years passed quietly, each step slow but sure. Andrew and Lelia grew to young adults and married. But Andrew's restlessness ultimately led to moving his young wife and baby, Andrew Jr., to Lexington, Massachusetts, to serve as apprentice to his silversmith uncle, Wesley. Here, Mac's father found deep satisfaction in putting his artistic talents to work creating beautiful designs in silver and pewter.

The adjustment to city life had not been easy for Lelia, but she endured it silently, content to see her young husband so happy with his work. When Mac was five and Roger was two, the family moved to Barleyville, South Carolina. This move was a compromise between city life and home. Here they were close enough to Iron Mountain to visit their families often. Not that Barleyville could have been considered a city by any stretch of the imagination, but the tiny village was a good location for the young Macklins.

Jessica had learned this story over the past two and a half years. Each new facet only endeared Mac's family to her more. While life in this new land was far from easy and not often pleasant, Jessica knew their strength to endure lay in their strong family ties and deep faith in God. She had prayed many prayers of thanks for this family. Coupled with her own loving family, she couldn't help wondering why she had been so blessed.

Listening to the women sitting and chatting over their work, Jessica caught sight of Oskati standing just across the green. He seemed to be involved in a heated discussion with another more heavyset young man whose arms were crossed in a pose of angry indignance. Jess remembered him from two years before. It was Bear Paw, Little Sparrow's brother.

Bear Paw and Little Sparrow were the children of Quiet Bear's brother-in-law, Elkinau, who had lived with an aggressive people in a neighboring Cherokee village to the north. Elkinau had been killed in a fight with White settlers, and Quiet Bear had taken in the children of his sister as was the Cherokee way.

For the past sixteen years, however, this tiny faction had simmered in bitterness. They warned the rest of the village to be alert, that their tiny hideaway was not invincible, and they constantly derided the original villagers for accepting many of the White ways brought to them by the Macklins.

Jess had wondered why these newcomers had stayed if they had been so dissatisfied with everything. Mac had only smiled when she asked, and commented that they may not have liked the way things were done in the village, but they never turned away any food or lodging their brothers offered them in their time of need.

Now, watching these two young men, Jess prayed that the doomsayers would be proven wrong, that this tranquil little village would be able to go on enjoying its peace and quiet, undisturbed.

Her attention was distracted from the scene outside by a gentle tugging at her skirts. She looked down into two large black-brown eyes fringed by long black eyelashes. The round little face looked so solemn, but Jess thought it was the most beautiful face she had ever seen.

"Hello," she smiled, kneeling down beside the child.

The little girl shyly returned a smile.

"What's your name?" Jess asked softly.

The little girl, no more than two or three years old, stuck her finger in her mouth and blinked her big dark eyes at Jess.

"Her name is Sara."

Jess looked up to see a tall, slender young woman with fine features. Her black hair hung in two long, neat braids. Jess greeted her, "You're Adá, Oskati's wife! Hello."

"Little Sara has been very curious about you," the woman said. "Your husband is one of her favorite friends. She's trying to decide if you might be a friend, too."

"I'd like that very much, Sara." Jess touched the toddler's silky black hair gently.

"Uh-oh."

Jess looked up to see what had caused Adá's warning. Standing in the doorway was Little Sparrow. Her long black hair hung straight nearly to the middle of her back. Her buckskin dress, brightly embroidered with beads and shells in intricate patterns of leaves and geometric shapes, fit her sleek figure perfectly.

The attractive young woman approached. Standing before Jess, she tilted her head back haughtily and said, "Well, has the amazing Jessica come to save our village from her land-hungry brothers or is she here scouting for them?"

Adá angrily rebuked her in Cherokee. Little Sparrow's response was a disdainful smile. The piercing look from her black eyes never wavered, and Jess was suddenly reminded of the cold look of a hawk. She couldn't help thinking that this young woman had inappropriately been named Little Sparrow. She had the look of a predator, not a small, plain bird.

Ignoring Sparrow's taunting remark, Jessica clenched her fist behind her back. "It's nice to see you, too, Little Sparrow," she replied dryly.

"Bear Paw and Mitakiah have called for a Council meeting tonight," Little Sparrow announced boldly. "You should come. You might find it very interesting."

With that, the girl started to leave, but Jess's bracelet caught her eye. A dark expression crossed her face. When their eyes met again, there was such a fierceness there that Jess was taken aback. Little Sparrow turned and stormed out of the meetinghouse without another word.

"Whew," Jess finally sighed as she looked at Adá who was still watching the door.

"You must be very careful, Rea' na tani," Adá soberly warned. "She can be very spiteful."

"Thank you for the warning. You're probably right." She bent down once more in response to a little tug at her hand. "Yes? What is it, Sara?"

Shyly, the little girl motioned for her mother to bend down, then whispered something in her ear. Adá smiled and stroked her child's silky, black hair. "She'd like to know if she could say hello to your horse."

"Of course," Jess replied with delight. "Would you like to go now?"

Little Sara nodded enthusiastically.

The three walked to the stables where Lady was quartered. Sara was delighted when Jess put her up on the sleek chestnut mare's back and led her around the small corral.

The Indian mother smiled fondly, watching her tiny daughter. "Oskati has promised her a pony of her own when she's a little older. She's been waiting to pet her since you rode in the other day."

Before coming to the valley, these Cherokee people had generally traveled afoot. Grandfather Macklin had always loved horses and had bought two sturdy draft horses to pull their wagon shortly after arriving in the colonies. He had encouraged the Cherokee to trade furs and deer skins, two things highly prized by the English, for a few good horses. As a result, over the years they had developed a good selection of saddle horses as well as draft animals.

The two women and Sara spent the rest of the morning chatting and getting acquainted. Jessica was elated to have made new friends, and she was beginning to feel more and more at home.

Oskati's wife told her that although things appeared normal, everyone was packed and ready to leave at a moment's notice. They were waiting for Mac's return before moving the families to High Meadow. While the villagers had confidence in young Macklin, they had seen many examples of a lack of regard for Indian claims.

Adá frowned. "Oskati wants to wait until Mac returns for the Council to meet. Bear Paw and Mitakiah are troublemakers; they like to stir up the bitterness of those who lost their land before."

That night at the Council meeting, Jessica saw the truth in Adá's words. Quiet Bear and four other elders sat solemnly at the head of the crowded room as Oskati and Bear Paw debated one another. The longer the exchange went on, the more heated it became. Oskati called for calm and reason, entreating the people to wait until Mac returned to find out what the new state leaders had to say.

Bear Paw reacted with contempt directed at the new American states and their leaders. Knowing Mac's popularity with the majority of his people, Bear Paw referred to him by his Cherokee name, River Walker, and was careful to portray his efforts as well-meaning, but futile.

Walking back and forth with slow deliberate steps and speaking in a low intense voice, he said, "No matter how well River Walker speaks, the White leaders will not listen to him. They will not because the blood of the Delaware flows within him. These intruders think because we've become Christians and abandoned our old beliefs, that we will meekly stand with bowed head as they murder us one by one, just as they've done at the mission in Pennsylvania."

A murmuring crept through the crowd in reaction to Bear Paw's words. Feeling the successful impact of his oratory, the Indian continued, raising his voice gradually. "When they come to take our land, they will have a surprise waiting. We will not allow it to happen here! I say we rise up with our weapons like Gideon of the ancient days. We will smite them down before they reach our valley. We will protect our homes and our families. They will know they cannot come here again!" His final words came in such vehement shouts that several of the younger men stood with raised fists and shouts of accord.

Oskati turned to the Council with one last plea. After the crowd had quieted a moment, he began gravely. "Brother Bear Paw is convincing, but I beg you to consider

66

the price. He would have us ride to the attack outside our valley, destroying the settlers before they even move against us. This action would surely set the militia and the state against us. They would see it as an attack by treacherous savages, not as an attempt by ordinary men to defend their homes.

"I say wait. Wait until River Walker returns with news of what's really happening." Oskati leveled a steady gaze at his opponent. "Then, if there's no other way, I will join you in the front of the battle in defense of our land. We'll stand at the middle of the valley and fight. But we will not attack outside."

Another murmur swept through the crowd. Jess could see the obviously divided feeling in the group. Anyone could understand the urgency of preventing their homes from being destroyed. But if they attacked outside their valley, reprisal would be quick and certain. It would be the perfect excuse for the state militia to move in and clear the valley for White settlement.

After Oskati had taken his place on the front row, the five Council members spoke quietly among themselves. Finally Quiet Bear stood. "My sister's son, Bear Paw, speaks with great passion but also deep bitterness. He would be a great warrior, if we were a warring people. But we are farmers now—men of peace. We will wait until River Walker returns. The news he brings will tell us whether we'll have to fight or not. This is the decision of the Council. Go home now and pray that the Almighty will protect our peace."

Adá and Jessica exchanged looks of relief. As the meeting began to disperse, Oskati joined them. Jess complimented him, but he only replied, "Just pray that Mac brings encouraging news."

As they spoke, Jess caught sight of Little Sparrow. She was standing with Bear Paw and two other young Indians. Their grim, hate-filled expressions sent a cold wave of dread over her, for she could imagine their faces painted for war. It was obvious they were in favor of Bear Paw's solution. She quickly diverted her attention back to her friends.

Little Sara had fallen asleep in her mother's arms during the meeting. Jess patted the chubby little hand gently as she said good-night to her two new friends.

Stepping outside, she drew her cloak around her shoulders as she walked along the path to the Macklins' cabin. The chill air of the fall night was clean and crisp, and Jessica breathed in deeply. Its freshness was a pleasant contrast to the closeness of the crowded meetinghouse. She walked slowly all alone, watching the myriad of stars twinkling brightly in the black velvet sky above.

In the past, she had spent many hours of her free time in solitude, riding or walking the hills of Cheltenham Farms. The only girl her age in the sparsely populated area had lived over ten miles away. Although she and Robbie had always been close, they had different interests. Robbie was the scholar of the family, devouring any book he could get his hands on. Jess had always loved the animals, especially the horses, and the minute her household chores were complete she would be down at the corrals or stables with her father and brother or tagging after her brother and Evan Collingsworth, Robbie's best friend.

She and Evan had been engaged before the war, but before they could marry he had been killed at Savannah during the same battle that claimed Mac's brother, Roger. In the two years between Evan's death and meeting Mac, Jessica had known loneliness, but that feeling had been slight compared to how she felt now. Without Mac near, she knew a loneliness so acute it was nearly overwhelming. Her thoughts constantly turned to him.

Mac should be returning tomorrow. She longed to see him, to be held in his strong embrace. Being in love and loving someone so very much could have its painful moments. It was the age-old paradox: Love could cause exquisite joy or the most shattering despair, occasionally at the same time.

Jessica stepped lightly onto the porch and entered the cabin to find Gran reading beside the fireplace. She had stayed at home with her husband who wasn't strong enough to attend the meeting. Gran didn't want to influence the group, but she had encouraged Jessica to accept Little Sparrow's spiteful invitation and go.

As Jess related the events of the meeting, she asked Gran about Bear Paw's allegations concerning mission Indians murdered in Pennsylvania.

Gran clasped her hands in anguish. "Mac didn't tell you? Of course not, it's just too horrible. We think some of his mother's distant relatives may have been there."

Jess sat down and murmured, "Oh, no."

Gran reached for her hand, continuing, "About a month ago, a friend stopped by with the dreadful news. I told Mac about it in the letter, and it upset him terribly—the senselessness and cruelty of it."

Jessica's heart sank. "What happened?"

Gran began reluctantly, "It seems some raiding Senecas were hiding close by the Moravian mission after an attack on one of the settlements. The White settlers in the area had been unhappy about the mission all along so they used the excuse to go in and search for the raiders. They—oh, I can't bear to tell it all . . . every one of the Delaware were killed." Tears filled Gran's eyes as she shook her head sadly.

Jess caught her breath, nearly choking on the lump in her throat.

After a long moment, Gran continued. "Jessica, terrible, terrible things have been done by both settlers and Indians. The atrocities have been so horrible on both sides that neither side takes time to stop and think. Most of the settlers label all Indians as inhuman savages, never considering that many Indians hate the killing as much as they do. And the retaliation continues.

"I pray Mac will have good news when he returns. There's so much bounty in this land; there must be a way to share it peacefully."

As much as Jess wanted to believe Gran's dream, she knew that people escaping the hunger-ridden, filthy, and crowded cities of the Old World were desperate for the freedom and wealth of land in America. The blame came when greed took over.

Now she understood what Mac had kept from telling her. Along with wanting to shield her from this terrible news, Jess knew he was having a difficult time accepting the barbarity committed against innocent people just because they were Indians. It had been especially disgusting in this case because the Whites had taken advantage of the fact the Indians at the mission were Christians and had not taken up arms in their own defense.

Jess couldn't help but think about the stark contrast between the ideals of the War for Independence and what was happening here. The dream was to establish a country where a man could have the freedom to make a home for himself and his family without fear of injustice and tyranny. The situation threatening the Iron Mountain

Cherokee was a blatant breach of that quest for just treatment for all.

Jess could hardly accept the hate and bitterness of Bear Paw and his followers because it led to the much publicized atrocities along the frontier. On the other hand, Oskati's position to stand and fight to defend their village was beyond reproach.

The thought that Mac would stand with his friends filled Jess with dread for his safety, yet she knew it was a situation he couldn't back away from. As much as she detested the bloodshed of warfare, she also knew that there came a time when people had to take a stand against injustice.

7

"Let him do the talking," Samuel Hampton grumbled to himself as he pulled his coat collar up against the cold autumn rain drizzling down his neck. "Why should I always let him do the talking?"

The rickety two-wheeled wooden cart jolted and lurched along the muddy ruts of the village street. Peering from beneath the dripping brim of his hat, he watched the swishing tail of the burro pulling the cart. Twice the contrary creature had bolted for no apparent reason, hurtling the pitiful excuse for a cabriolet into a teeth-rattling ride over bumps and through mud puddles. Each time, Hampton had been certain the whole cart would fly apart before the burro decided to slow down to a sane pace. Hampton's driving ability had little to do with controlling the creature's unpredictable behavior.

"I'll arrange my own transport next time," he assured himself as he glanced glumly at George Melden riding ahead on a sturdy black gelding.

Without turning in the saddle or calling back to Hampton, Melden pointed to the side of the road where two horses stood before a building with candles aglow in the windows. It was too dark to read the sign swinging above the door, but after numerous small villages with similar buildings, he knew it must be the local tavern. Since leaving the cobblestone streets of Charleston over a week ago, he was beginning to feel the rugged miles traveling in the cabriolet and knew they were beginning to take their toll.

It had been a nerve-wracking experience trying to get through Charleston without drawing undue attention to themselves. Melden had arranged for their transportation at a small stable on the west side of the city. When asked whether he wanted to ride a horse or drive a buggy, Hampton had watched the many fine carriages and shays passing by and there was no question which mode of travel he preferred. He hadn't been prepared for the two-wheeled cart pulled by a sway-backed pony that Melden brought out for him. The security agent had squelched his objections with a sharp rebuke not to make a fuss or people might begin to question them about their national loyalties.

Using the map that attorney Harold Smythe had sent with his letter, they left Charleston the next day to travel northwest toward a place called Ellensgate, South Carolina. The sway-backed pony had gone lame yesterday, and Melden had traded it for this cantankerous burro.

They'd been traveling for eight days. Earlier that day a farmer along the road had told them that their destination would take another three days. As he climbed down from the creaking cart, Hampton's stomach growled from hunger and his bones ached from the punishing ride. His feet sank ankle deep in the mud next to the cart, and he struggled clumsily to slog his way to the stone step in front of the tavern door. When his muddy foot slipped off the edge of the step causing him to stumble, he was too miserable even to care about the look of disdain Melden cast his way. The young man had become so used to seeing the reflection of Melden's low opinion in his haughty face, it had ceased to disturb him.

The dimly lit tavern was so run down, Hampton was glad the lighting wasn't better so he couldn't see the dirt and grime he felt sure covered every surface in the place. Their dinner of squirrel stew and rock-hard biscuits was less than appetizing, but Melden found a particular liking to the ale provided by the proprietor.

Hampton managed to drink half a cupful of the stout mead, but the stew unsettled his stomach. Although the ale seemed to warm him, the young Englishman asked for a cup of tea instead. The barmaid, a large woman, studied him with a critical eye but brought him the tea without comment.

This particular night, Hampton noticed that his companion was drinking more than usual, and it made him a little uneasy. The agent was sullenly quiet during their meal but that was not unusual. His sarcastic remarks about Hampton being a spoiled schoolboy had become boring and since they no longer drew comments from his young traveling companion, he had little else to say.

Before long, two men came in and sat down to greet the proprietor boisterously. They were soon joined by a third man, coming in out of the rain, who stamped his boots noisily.

"Hello, Sergeant," the barmaid called over the rough plank that served as the bar. "What can I get for our hero tonight?"

"Evenin', Miss Betty. Just bring me a pint to warm this old carcass, and bring it quick."

"Hero," Melden smirked, hunching over his mug of ale.

Hampton was relieved to see that the others had not heard the sarcastic remark. But he became more nervous by the moment as he realized his associate was totally in the grip of the strong ale. Melden's confident businesslike demeanor had been replaced by a dark, primitive mood that could only mean trouble.

The three men at the other table chattered good-naturedly for a few minutes. When a second helping of ale was served, one of the men stood and declared, "Lift your glasses, men, to the Continental rangers. We twisted them cowardly redcoat tails and sent 'em scurryin' back to their mamas!"

"Here, here!" the other two joined in enthusiastically.

Fully aware of Melden's intoxicated state, Hampton watched the husky man closely. Slowly the agent straightened himself up and rose from his chair. Even in the dim lighting Hampton could see a definite glazed look in Melden's eyes.

"Melden?" he asked apprehensively. "What are you doing?"

"Nobody who hides behind a tree shootin' at proper soldiers doin' their proper duty, can call us 'cowardly.'" With that Melden turned toward the three men, his words growing from a low growl to a thunderous roar.

The student's heart began to pound furiously as he watched in stunned silence as the scene unfolded before him. Melden picked up the chair he'd been sitting in and promptly broke it over the shoulders of one of the locals. Hampton jumped out of the way as one of the others picked up his chair and sailed it through the air at the attacker. In less than five minutes, both tables had been shattered, the plank bar split in two, one of the men thrown through a window, and a stack of pewter mugs scattered across the room.

Melden had just picked up the sergeant and was holding him in a crushing bear hug when Miss Betty emerged from the back room carrying a huge iron skillet. The loud clang across Melden's head was followed by a groan and then a thudding crash as the agent collapsed across the one remaining chair untouched during the melee.

The woman spun around toward Hampton with her skillet poised and ready, but he held up his hands in a signal of surrender. Looking about the room, he decided that a whirlwind could not have caused any more destruction.

With a sinking feeling, the nephew began wondering if all the horror stories he'd heard about the wild American frontier were true. If so, the very least they could expect would be tar and feathers, possibly even boiling in oil. The boy's expectations were not brightened when the man who had been thrown through the window staggered back in and announced, "Put that man in irons and drag him down to the jail."

Freed from Melden's bear hug, the sergeant stared down at the unconscious hulk sprawled in the midst of the debris. "Yessiree, Sheriff, with pleasure," he grinned breathlessly.

In a few minutes, the three men had dragged Melden out. Hampton stood in the middle of the shattered furnishings unable to believe what he'd just seen.

"Well, you gonna help me clean up this mess?" Miss Betty asked with her hands propped on her ample hips.

The Englishman dared not refuse and nodded, still slightly dazed. He spent an exhausting hour picking up broken furniture and restacking the mugs on another plank that had been brought in. Miss Betty seemed to take pity on him, however, and told him that the rooms at the inn were all filled, but he could sleep in the storeroom if he wanted to. Thankful not to be turned out in the rain, he accepted. A moth-eaten blanket was all he had to keep out the damp chill while he slept on an old cot in the cubbyhole room behind the kitchen.

The next morning, Hampton awoke with a cough and aching head. After a breakfast of strong coffee and biscuits, he went down to the jail to find out Melden's fate and see when they would be able to leave.

"Harold Smythe, ya' say?" the sheriff asked when Hampton explained the purpose of their journey.

"Yes," he replied, glancing over his shoulder. He could see Melden sitting on the edge of a low cot holding his head, still ringing from last night.

Hampton produced the documents and after the sheriff had pored over them for a time, the officer looked at Hampton, then at Melden, then back at Hampton.

"I think it was the war, sir," Hampton spoke in a hushed tone so Melden couldn't hear. "It must have done something to his mind. You know, losing a war can do that to a soldier, especially losing to a country that's so . . ." He stopped himself when he saw the sheriff watching him closely. "Young," he finally concluded diplomatically. "Mr. Melden's usually quite calm, but he just drank a little too much last night, and . . . well, you know the rest."

The sheriff pursed his lips and drummed on his desk a few moments as he studied Hampton. "I'm also the judge," he said, picking up a wooden mallet on the desk. He banged it down once and declared, "Guilty as charged, three days in jail and however much it takes to repair and replace the fine furnishin's of the tavern."

Hampton held his breath, fearing any additional sentence might include something about a gallows.

"Now, lad, I'd suggest you find yourself somethin' worthwhile to do for a few days if you're gonna wait around for him. And after he gets outta here, you better be sure to keep him away from strong drink. Next time he may not find so merciful a judge."

Hampton nodded and hurried out the door. Once outside, he leaned against the building and let out a long sigh of relief.

"From now on, I'll do the talking," he mumbled grimly.

8

Mac had been gone for two nights. On the second night, Jessica had a difficult time sleeping. Although her body was weary, she couldn't turn off the thoughts whirling in her head. She missed Mac so much she could hardly stand it. Her joy over the prospect of his return was clouded by her uneasiness over the problem facing the people of the village and Mac's grandparents. She finally slept for a few hours but awoke early, feeling just as tired as she was the night before.

Jess was very encouraged to find that Grandfather Macklin was well enough to come to the table for breakfast. Visiting over fresh apple muffins, she mentioned a story Mac had told her about the first time he went camping by himself and asked how his parents had felt when the sudden storm came up.

"Ah yes, lass. We prayed all night for his safety. When the storm finally abated in the morn', Andrew and Quiet Bear went alookin' for 'im. They searched high and low. When they found his bedroll snagged on a tree root at the edge of the river, they feared the worst.

"'Twas about that time, they caught the aroma of cooking meat. They came to a wee glen, and there was the lad sittin' beside a small cookin' fire roastin' a rabbit he'd snared! He served 'em breakfast! Needless to say, we were all mighty proud of 'im and thankful to the good Lord for keepin' him in his care.

"That was the time he received his Cherokee name, River Walker, because he had walked above the raging river without harm. It was a miracle that he'd been able to climb that cliff above the river and reach the cave where he took shelter."

Gran told her about the difficulty Mac and Roger had after their father died.

"They were such good lads," she reminisced with a dreamy smile. "It was very hard for them to accept the loss of Lelia and little Jamie, yet they seemed to understand the tremendous pain their father felt without their mother. The boys were somehow able to let him go a bit easier when he became ill. They knew their parents had been reunited in heaven.

"Young Mac had to grow up very quickly then. He was always a steady boy and as soon as he could, he decided to learn a trade to support them. He went to serve an apprenticeship at silversmithing with his Uncle Wesley, just as his father had done."

"Aye, he's always been a stable lad, but he had a sharp wit, and he was a bit of a tease, too," Grandfather put in, his eyes twinkling with delight.

"Remember the time, Mother, that he and Roger had old Joseph convinced he'd turned Mac into a toadstool?"

"Good gracious, yes," Gran laughed. "Joseph was an old Natiri gentleman taken as a slave during one of the clan wars. Somehow he ended up here and decided to stay.

"His father had been a shaman and Joseph claimed to have his powers. The poor fellow was so cross he was always threatening to turn the children into toadstools. He frightened wee Jamie so one time he refused to leave the house. The lad was only four—let's see, that means Roger was ten and Mac twelve. Well, the two older boys were put out that their little brother had been frightened like that, and they decided to do something about it.

"Some children were playing by the old man's door, and he came hurrying out to frighten them away. Roger and Mac strolled by, and Joseph yelled at them as well. Mac called back that he shouldn't be so cross. This impudence only made old Joseph angrier, and he threatened to turn Mac into a toadstool! Mac dared him, and the old Indian started stomping and cursing in his dialect.

"Mac suddenly grabbed his head, yelled, and began running around in circles as if he were mad. Then he ran toward the forest. Roger rushed after him and came back a little later carrying a toadstool and accusing old Joseph of destroying his brother. Of course, Mac was close by and when Joseph denied it, Mac began crying a wee call of help from his hiding place. The sound seemed to be coming from the plant in Roger's hand, and the old fellow became so frightened of his own powers, he swore never to do such a thing again. He was afraid of the blood vengeance that might be directed against him. The boys planned to go to him the next morning and confess, but Joseph moved out in the night."

"Oh dear," Jess grinned ruefully. "What happened to him?"

"We were quite concerned until we heard that he'd joined a group of settlers as a guide into the Ohio Valley.

"Andrew disciplined the boys for their prank, but everyone in the village, especially the children, were relieved that the old man had gone. He had really been a very disagreeable person."

"Who?"

Their heads turned to see Mac's tall, broad-shouldered silhouette standing against the morning sunlight streaming in the doorway.

"Mac!" Jess cried with glee as she jumped up and hurried to his open arms. They held each other tightly. "We weren't expecting you 'til noon," she said, breathless with delight.

"I couldn't wait to get back. After a short rest, Ettinsmoor and I rode half the night. Did you get my note?" he asked her quietly.

She loved the sound of his deep, rich voice with its slight Scottish burr. "Yes, and the bracelet." She held up her hand for his approval. "It's wonderful."

He kissed her forehead, and arm in arm they joined his grandparents at the table.

"Sit down. I'll bring you some coffee," Jess directed.

After kissing his grandmother's cheek, Mac grasped his grandfather's shoulder. "I knew they couldn't keep you down for long," he said with a broad smile. "Sounds like I got back just in time. Now, at least I'll be able to defend myself and make sure you don't tell Jess all the bad stories about my growing years."

"We have no bad stories about you, dear." Gran lovingly clasped his hand across the table.

"Well, there was that time—" Grandfather began.

"James," his wife chided.

Jess filled everyone's cups.

"Well, laddie, don't beat around the bush now," Grandfather urged. "What have you found out?"

Mac began with a note of optimism, "Do you remember Franklin Barton, my friend from Barleyville?"

"Yes, the young doctor who attended your wedding," Gran answered.

"Since his war wounds cost him the use of his left arm, his medical career has become a political career. Thankfully for us, he's been appointed a regional representative to the South Carolina Assembly. He was in Camden, and I was able to talk to him about the problem here. He assured me that with all of the Indian uprisings along the northwestern borders, many in the Assembly want to slow down the rush of settlers into Indian lands here. They don't especially want the Cherokee uprisings to start again.

"But it seems that the Fair View Land Company and Carlson Frye do have a connection with a couple of the representatives from Charleston. That's apparently where the papers they brought came from. Franklin's looking into it for us and feels certain he can appeal their claims and keep them from forcing the sale."

"That's wonderful, Andrew dear," Gran exclaimed with joy.

Jess held her enthusiasm in check. She could sense that Mac had something more to say—something he wasn't happy about.

His grandfather saw it too. "What is it that's concerning you so, lad?" he asked bluntly.

Mac sighed. "Franklin's appeal will take time."

"Go on," Grandfather urged.

"On the way back I crossed the trail of probably ten to fifteen wagons headed this way."

"You mean they're on their way already?" Jess asked in surprise.

"Looks that way."

Just then a knock sounded at the door. Gran opened it to find Quiet Bear and Oskati standing there. Mac greeted them both with a firm handshake and answered their questioning glances with the information he had just shared.

"So, it appears that Bear Paw and Mitakiah may have their battle after all," Quiet Bear responded gloomily.

"Let's not get the war paint out just yet, Quiet Bear. I followed the trail to a campsite on Willowby Creek. That's a good three days traveling time for the settlers' wagons and stock. If we leave within the hour, we can reach them just after they make camp this evening."

"What are you suggesting, Mac?" Oskati asked curiously.

"I say we ask the Council to authorize the three of us and maybe one more to ride out and talk with them—tell them what the situation is here. They may not even realize this land is already occupied. Some of these land speculators can be a little sparing with the truth and strong on promoting their parcels of territory."

"Oskati," Grandfather said, "have the boys ready the cabriolet, and I'll come along."

Gran glanced at Mac anxiously.

"Grandfather," Mac said quietly. "The ride in that two-wheeled cart can shake a body apart. May I have your permission to speak with the settlers on your behalf?"

"Andrew, you said they can't keep me down for long. I'd like to go with you." The old gentleman stood defiantly then began weaving a bit unsteadily. Jess was instantly by his side, helping him back to his chair.

84

"James dear," Gran implored, "you're still weak from being in bed so long. Please let Andrew speak for you."

"Perhaps you're right," he replied in dismal acquiescence to his wife's words.

"We'll need you here, my friend," Quiet Bear assured him, laying his hand on Grandfather Macklin's shoulder. "Someone must stay and keep Bear Paw from stirring things up while we're gone. The people will listen to you."

9

There had been uncharacteristically little rain in the mountains the past two weeks causing small clouds of dust to swirl about the party of four horsemen as they rode at a steady pace toward the gap. In this transitional time between summer and winter, it was as if the season was trying to decide whether to ease into the cold of winter or hang on tightly to the heat of summer. The autumn morning air had been quite chill, but now as the sun was climbing toward its apex in the cloudless sapphire blue, the day had become very warm.

Mac was riding a large sorrel belonging to Oskati. He had left his own thoroughbred, Ettinsmoor, at the village to rest after his long journey to Camden. Oskati rode next to him followed by Quiet Bear.

Tall Tree, another member of the Council, accompanied them. He represented that faction of the village in favor of attacking the settlers before they reached the valley.

At the hastily called Council meeting following Mac's return, his news of the approaching group of settlers had caused great consternation. Mac favored Tall Tree coming along because he knew him to be a fair man, and Bear Paw's friends would accept Tall Tree's account of the meeting without suspicion.

As they rode, Mac's thoughts turned to Jessica. He could still see her standing on his grandparents' porch, the golden sunlight glistening in a coppery shine on her soft chestnut brown hair. Her lovely face had been so serious in concern for him. "I wish you'd take a little time to rest before you go," she had said. Securing the saddlebags to the saddle, he had reassured her he would rest that night when they made camp on their way back.

With hands on her hips and a slightly exasperated smile, she asked, "Do you suppose there'll ever be a time when we're not having to say good-bye every time we turn around?"

Turning, he took her in his arms and held her close. "Someday, Jess . . . surely someday. We should be back before noon tomorrow. Quiet Bear has given the order for the women and children to move to High Meadow. I'll see you there. It's not home, but you'll be safe."

With that, their lips met in a lingering good-bye, and he rode off to join the other three.

Now he couldn't help wondering if there would ever come a time of being able to work peacefully in his shop listening to Jess singing softly as she busily took care of their home. He still found himself marveling that the love shining in her eyes was really meant for him. Still uneasy about her being here at Iron Mountain, he couldn't deny how deeply he enjoyed her presence.

The trail took the four riders across the gently rolling meadowland of the valley stretching some twenty miles along a great cleft near the southern end of the Appalachian chain. It was an isolated area with only a narrow gap to the north allowing accessibility by wagon. The mountainsides rising from the valley floor were mantled in a rich array of hardwoods. The red-golds, yellows, and oranges of the hickories, birches, and poplars stood out in bright patches against the dark green of hemlock, spruces, and fir growing farther up the slopes and along the ridges.

Wide areas of what appeared to be meadow clearings were in reality heaths of rhododendron bushes, greenbriars, and mountain laurel. In the spring they would be adorned with flaming reds and pinks and snowy white blossoms innocently masking the nearly impenetrable snares of branches and roots.

The four men stopped to rest their mounts for brief intervals, and continuing to travel steadily, they reached the entrance to the valley two hours before sundown. Following the well-worn trail for another hour, they finally arrived at the campsite. Keeping alert, they dismounted and cautiously led their horses to the outside circle of the fifteen wagons Mac had seen earlier.

"H-e-l-l-o in the camp," Mac called.

"State your business, stranger," came a gruff voice from the other side of the nearest wagon.

"Name's Andrew Macklin. We're from the Iron Mountain settlement up ahead in the Chalequah Valley. We'd like to talk to the man in charge of your party."

Holding an old French musket, the gentleman with the gruff voice stepped out from behind the wagon prepared to fire.

"I'm Tobias Alder. We'll talk outside the circle if it's all the same to you. We've had a bit of trouble from a band of Creeks, and everyone's a touch nervous." Alder stepped forward. Clad in a shirt of homespun with dark breeches, he was a short, squarish-built man with gray hair tied back in a queue at the nape of his neck. His steel gray eyes shielded by bushy eyebrows watched as the four approached.

Through the space between wagons, Mac and his men could see that most of the people inside the protective circle seemed unaware of their presence. Two musket barrels protruded rather conspicuously, however, from the front and rear of the nearest wagon.

"We're a bit curious about your destination, Mr. Alder," Mac began.

"What business would that be of yours?" Alder squinted suspiciously.

Mac knew he had to judge this man correctly. Alder looked more like a shopkeeper than a wagonmaster and although he was apparently able to use his musket, he seemed uncomfortable with it. Mac watched him closely.

"My grandparents are the missionaries at the Iron Mountain settlement," Mac began. "This is Quiet Bear, chief of the Cherokee Council, Tall Tree, also of the Council, and Oskati, one of the younger leaders. They've been approached by a Mr. Carlson Frye with the Fair View Land Company about selling the settlement land."

"Ahhh, that's different," Alder said as his attitude began to warm. "I guess that means you can tell us a little about the land we've bought."

Mac exchanged glances with his three grim-faced companions, then asked, "You've already bought the land? Do you have a map of the sections you purchased?"

"Certainly, just a moment. Stinson, fetch those maps out of my wagon."

One of the musket barrels disappeared.

"Our scouts tell us we'll be reaching the gap tomorrow morning," Alder went on. "It'll be a great relief to be at the end of our journey. We're a weary band, Mr. Macklin.

We've come all the way from Norfolk. Our homes were destroyed by a fire that swept up from the docks. We lost nearly everything. Those of us whose businesses were spared sold out and pooled our resources then started west. We'd had our fill of that crowded, rat-infested city existence, anyway."

The man named Stinson brought the packet holding the maps and handed it to Alder. "Here we are," Alder said.

Mac glanced briefly at the scout and thought he looked vaguely familiar. His wide jaw gave him the appearance of constantly gritting his teeth. His floppy hat was pulled low over his face and in the quick glimpse, Mac couldn't see the man's eyes.

Alder opened the map and proudly pointed to their destination. Tall Tree grumbled in disgust as Quiet Bear and Oskati looked at Mac with undisguised alarm in their eyes.

Immediately sensing something wrong, Alder asked warily, "What's the matter?"

"Well, Mr. Alder," Mac began, "the land you indicated encompasses three-fourths of the Iron Mountain village and fields. You've paid for land someone else still owns and occupies."

"That's impossible!" he snapped. "We've got proper legal deeds to that land."

Alder handed Mac some papers. He took them and read them carefully. They appeared in order. Then suddenly a name at the bottom caught his eye: Harold Smythe, attorney-at-law, Ellensgate, South Carolina.

"Mr. Alder, I'm afraid you've been victimized by some very clever land speculators. This land was never legally purchased from the people at the settlement. Did you actually deal with Harold Smythe?"

"Well . . . no. Frye handled the paperwork for us." Alder was weighing what Mac had just told him. At last he said with determination, "What you say is impossible. We haven't come all this way to be turned back at the door! Winter's coming on. We have families to prepare shelter for. We have a legal right to that land, and we mean to possess it!"

Alder stepped back a pace and again assumed a warning posture with his musket.

"Be reasonable, man. You can't expect the people at Iron Mountain to sit by calmly while you move in on their land." Mac realized that the sudden fear in Alder's eyes was born of desperation.

"It's not theirs anymore. Now, I think you'd better move on out of here."

Now the man's musket was in a ready position. Alder began stepping backwards toward the camp. "Go on back and tell 'em they better be out of the valley in two days 'cause we're coming on!"

Mac could see the futility of talking any more. He and his men retreated to their horses and mounted. They rode away from the camp, each one well aware of the dangerous situation rapidly developing.

They rode silently with their pace unhurried as each of them thought about the situation facing them. The uneasiness that had plagued Mac since receiving Gran's letter now deepened to solid dread, for they were faced with the grim reality of an impending conflict. No more speculation; the invaders were on the doorstep. Considering the exchange of words with Alder, Mac's hope for a reasonable solution to the situation failed.

They would make camp for the night by the Benedict River, the stream that cut through the valley a few miles the other side of the gap. It had recently been named after the traitorous Arnold because of its treacherous currents and flash flooding from rains in the high country despite fair weather in the valley.

Deep shadows were gathering in the trees on either side of the trail. It would be dark by the time they reached the river, but the way was well-known to each of them. In the waning light, the horses stepped along steadily, their hooves making the only sound in the stillness and raising little gray puffs of dust.

The fragrant calm air was growing cool. Mac glanced up toward the high ridges and the dark outline of fir trees along both sides of the gap, standing like bristles against the pale lavender light of the evening sky. Turning to Oskati, he decided to suggest that the best place to make a stand would be the gap itself. Suddenly out of the corner of his eye, he caught a movement beside a nearby tree.

Four musket shots instantly rang out, shattering the quiet. Panic-stricken whinnies echoed shrilly off the rocks and tree-lined walls in the gap. When the echoes died away, there was silence.

10

After Mac and the others had ridden away from the settlement, Jess stood for a long time watching them until their small forms were swallowed up in the rolling meadowland. She wasn't in the least superstitious but she couldn't escape the old Gaelic idea that if you watch someone leaving until they're out of sight, you will never see them again. She shivered slightly from a sudden grip of dread as the riders disappeared from view.

The last time she had felt such a strong sense of foreboding was just before she received news of Sir Gaston's serious illness. She and her brother had ridden to Ellensgate but failed to arrive in time to see him before his death. That had been a very sad time for her, and she still keenly missed their dear old family friend. Robbie had always been her protector as they were growing up, and she suddenly wished he were here now to accompany Mac. She was confident Mac could handle just about any situation, but if the meeting turned ugly, he might be outnumbered.

Her disquieted musing was interrupted by the jangling and creaking of an approaching harness and wagon. Turning, she saw Adá and little Sara in a buckboard stopping on the drive. Adá's brow was slightly furrowed as she glanced toward the cross-valley trail, so Jess didn't find it hard to guess what Oskati's young wife was thinking.

"They're going to be just fine," Jess said more enthusiastically than she intended, as if her saying it would make it so.

"Of course they are," Adá replied more vigorously than necessary. She continued rather absently, "We wondered if you'd like to ride to High Meadow with us."

"I hope I packed enough for their supper." Jess was lost in her own thoughts. "They'll be hungry tonight after that long ride . . . I'm sorry, Adá, what did you say?"

"Hmmm?" Adá was just as preoccupied as Jessica.

"Something about High Meadow?"

"Yes, Sara and I wondered if you'd like to ride with us to High Meadow."

Gran had stepped out onto the porch just after the wagon pulled up. She walked over and put her arm around Jessica's shoulders. "That's a very good idea, dear. You go on and ride with them."

"I thought I'd be driving your team for you and Grandfather," Jessica replied.

"That's all right, you go on ahead. We're going to stay here." Gran's face was lined with concern. She lowered her voice to a whisper, "I think it'd be too hard on James. He's still so weak. I'm not sure he could stand the strain of it."

Little more than an hour later, Jess stood beside Gran and waved good-bye to Adá, Sara, and the other women and children as the men moved their families to the safety of High Meadow.

"Mac'll be upset when he finds that you're not at High Meadow tomorrow, Jessica," Gran worried. "You should've gone."

Jess slipped her arm around Gran's waist and smiled, trying to lighten the mood. "Now, Gran, you know as well as I that beneath his serious stony exterior beats the tenderest of hearts. He may grumble a bit, but he'd really be upset if I went off and left you and Grandfather alone. Speaking of Grandfather, it's past lunchtime. I imagine he's famished. Don't you think it's a good sign his appetite is improving?"

"Oh, Jessica, you are a treasure!" Gran smiled, grateful for the cheerfulness whether a forced effort or not. As she watched the trail of Cherokee families move in a line toward the southern hills, she sighed deeply. "We thought we had found the perfect place when we settled here. Who would have ever thought that with the abundance of new land, anyone would want what is here. I guess there's not much else we can do now, is there."

Turning toward the house, she added, "Come in and after lunch I'll show you the scarf I'm making for your mother. Oh dear, I left my sewing basket down at the meetinghouse yesterday."

"I'll get it for you," Jess offered. "You go on in and see about Grandfather."

As Jess walked through the nearly deserted village, she didn't want to think about what might happen along these quiet little streets. She knew the frontier presented a wonderful opportunity for anyone with the courage and fortitude to carve out a new home. The hardships were numerous but so were the benefits of an independent, self-supporting life.

Unfortunately in many cases, this opportunity had encroached upon the vastly divergent societies of the Indians. Some of these groups looked upon war and killing as a glorious way of life. However, many more did not. How many times had Jessica heard her father comment that many could probably have lived peacefully, side by side, if it weren't for the unbridled greed of some of the European newcomers.

Jess had heard many gruesome stories of the atrocities committed by the Indians along the frontier. The conflicts were stirred up by the greed of some Whites and the implacable viciousness of those Indians who would not tolerate any invasion of their hunting ground. The ones caught in the middle were the people who were only looking for new beginnings—people seeking a decent place in which to raise their families. These fell prey to those warring Indians fighting for their homes.

The Indians who wanted to live peacefully were often blamed along with those who did not. These innocent Indians were not only plagued by settlers, they also suffered destruction and often exploitation as slaves from those tribes with whom they differed.

Jess knew the solution to this problem was beyond her comprehension, yet she couldn't help believing that in this tiny corner of the New World, it didn't have to be the way it was in other areas. Something should be able to be done to prevent bloodshed or the loss of the village.

The quiet padding of her slippered feet and the soft rustle of her skirts were the only sounds in the silence—a silence that was eerie and expectant. Jess had seen only a handful of men standing down at the corrals by the stable. She couldn't help but wonder how long the emptiness that permeated the village would last.

Once inside the meetinghouse, she found Gran's sewing basket sitting on a bench near the far window. All of a sudden voices outside startled her.

"Everything's going just as planned, my little vixen." A man with a crisp English accent was talking outside. "It won't be long now, and I'll be able to show you the wonders of the world."

"You should have waited until dark. Someone might have seen you." It was Little Sparrow. Her voice was cold and impersonal in contrast to the man's friendliness.

Jess tiptoed to the window deciding to risk a peek. She was stunned by what she saw: Howard Canfield was walking arm in arm with Little Sparrow!

As she watched them move away, Jess realized what had puzzled her before. Canfield's dress in frontier buckskins did not match his proper British accent and fair skin. But, an even more puzzling question was now at hand. Why was Carlson Frye's business partner meeting with Little Sparrow? The apprehension she had felt when she first met Canfield was magnified now by the realization that Little Sparrow and Canfield were somehow linked together. Individually, they presented an unpleasant element; together they might be a formidable adversary.

Jess looked at the sewing basket in her hand. A Bible verse had been intricately stitched into a corner of the fabric: "Where sin abounded, grace did much more abound" (Romans 5:20). The verse encouraged her heart as she thought about Gran and Grandfather and tried to dismiss the dangerous implications of this surprising alliance.

"Mr. Hampton, someone's here to see you."

The young man turned in his bed to look at the pretty young blonde talking.

"Who is it?" he moaned weakly.

"It's me," Melden said, entering the room brusquely. "How much longer are you going to languish abed, Hampton?"

"Mr. Hampton is still very weak," the woman defended, going to her patient's bedside.

"Well, he'd better gather his strength quickly. We must be on our way," Melden growled unsympathetically.

The patient looked up at the young lady standing protectively beside him. A tiny thing with a halo of golden curls framing a pixie-like face, bright blue eyes, and a ready smile, she had been the one bright spot in his whole dismal existence these past two months since leaving England. He certainly wasn't anxious to leave the comfort of his sickbed with such an attractive and sympathetic nurse to attend him.

"Will you excuse us, please, Miss?" Melden nodded politely.

As she looked at the young man, still quite pale, her admiration and concern were obvious. He nodded to assure her he would be all right. Smiling back, she left the room with a grim frown directed toward Melden.

"I'm sure your uncle would be most upset if he knew you were malingering here simply to capture the attentions of the doctor's daughter."

Melden's six-foot frame seemed to tower over Hampton's bed. His broad stern face reminded the young man of a fierce viking. His powdered wig and well-cut suit of clothes looked a bit incongruous with his size and rough features, especially with the bruises from his recent tavern fight still faintly visible.

No longer was Hampton intimidated by the burly agent. He quickly repudiated the accusation. "If you'll remember correctly, Melden, it was *you* who delayed us for three days after that ridiculous brawl. If I hadn't had to wait at that filthy inn in that squalid little village for you to be released from jail, I wouldn't have caught the ague. Even then, as bad as I felt, I pressed on, didn't I? Pressed on, traveling until so wracked with fever I didn't even know my own name. Can I help it that I collapsed short of our destination? Granted, the doctor and his daughter have been most kind, but do you think I've enjoyed being ill and confined to bed in this wretched wilderness?"

Hampton's visitor looked toward the door with a slightly suspicious smile curling one corner of his mouth. "I'm sure it has been a trying experience," he added. "All that aside, I have news for you that had better speed up your recovery."

"What is it?" Hampton asked impatiently.

"I told you we weren't far from Ellensgate. It's only about twenty miles west of here."

"And why should that bit of news hasten my recovery?" Hampton asked petulantly as he smoothed the covers over himself.

Melden's pale blue eyes reflected his disdain for the curator's nephew as he folded his powerful arms across his broad chest. "I was speaking with the innkeeper over a pint just now. We were just chatting about this and that when he mentioned that he was originally from the south of England not far from Cheltenham."

Hampton was only half listening, thankful that Melden had not been drinking too much again. Melden continued. "He said a bloke from Cheltenham named Canfield has been through here several times since May."

"What?" The young man bolted upright, forgetting his weakened condition. "Is he certain? How does he know for sure? Perhaps it's another Canfield."

"The first time he was through here in May, he was asking for directions to Harold Smythe's office in Ellensgate."

Hampton sank back against his pillow, closing his eyes and rubbing his forehead in dismay. "I don't suppose you could go on ahead to Ellensgate, and I could follow in a few days when I've regained my strength?"

When no reply came, the young Englishman opened one eye to see Melden standing there, arms akimbo, looking down at him. The impatience reflected in the security agent's viking-like face had hardened to disgust.

Sighing, Hampton murmured, "No, I don't suppose you could."

With any luck, the patient thought he could probably muster enough strength to travel to Ellensgate, see Miss McClaren or Mrs. Macklin, whichever the case might be by now, and make it back to Dr. Nelson's home in time to die in the arms of the lovely Lucianna.

11

Jess spent another restless night, tossing and turning. Pulling Mac's pillow closer and hugging it didn't help allay the deep uneasiness inside.

She finally rose from bed, wrapped her shawl about her shoulders, and went out into the main room. After adding more wood to the glowing coals in the large fireplace, she filled the coffeepot with water from the large wooden water keg.

James Macklin had always been something of an inventor, and he had constructed an ingenious method for directing water right up to the kitchen window. Whenever they needed to fill the water keg, they simply laid one end of a narrow flue in a gurgling pool at the cold spring that flowed down the mountainside some sixty feet from the house. The other end of the flue was attached to a small framework just outside the kitchen window. Leather hinges joined two thirty-foot sections of wooden trough, each about five inches across. One person would stand on the outside with two large piggins, wooden buckets with a paddle-like handle on one side. When one piggin was filled, someone passed it through the window to another person waiting on the inside to pour it into the water keg.

This step-saver became more and more appreciated as the elderly couple found it increasingly difficult to climb up to the spring and carry the heavy buckets down. Each day Quiet Bear's two young grandnephews would come by and fill the water keg for their friends.

The sky was beginning to streak with the first gray light when the coffee was finished. The morning air was chilly and Jess knew that the first frost was near. She poured some coffee and warmed her hands around the steaming cup. Just as she sat down next to the warmth of the fire, she heard a scuffing noise on the porch. She got up and was reaching for the heavy latch when it raised of its own accord.

Jess stepped back, her heart pounding, as the door swung open. The yellow glow from the fireplace washed over three men; one man was being supported by the other two. The woman was stunned and for a moment stood frozen, motionless.

"Jess, get some water and bandages." It was Mac's voice.

She hurried to do his bidding as he and Oskati carried Quiet Bear into their bedroom.

"What happened?" she asked as she returned with the water and clean linen cloths.

Mac was bent over Quiet Bear, cutting away his blood-soaked shirt. He and Oskati had pressed a wad of material against the wound in an attempt to stop the bleeding. Jess turned away, nearly swooning, as Mac removed the wadding from the terrible wound.

Mac's dirt-smudged face was pale, his jaw set grimly in stony silence. The intense anger smoldering in his dark eyes frightened Jessica.

Oskati slumped in the chair in the corner of the room, his buckskin hunting shirt torn and bloodstained. Jess turned to him and knelt beside him. Taking a deep breath, she began to examine his injury. Although he had lost a lot of blood, Oskati's wound was not serious. The musket ball had passed cleanly through the upper arm, missing the bone. In comparison to Quiet Bear's horrible wound, his was not bad and Jess's dizziness passed quickly.

"What happened, Oskati?" she whispered in dismay.

He looked at her blankly, exhausted and weak. Finally, he gathered his senses as Jess administered to the flesh wound in his left arm.

"We were ambushed. We had no warning . . . no warning! It was so quiet, so peaceful. They were there at the gap, lying in wait. Tall Tree never knew what hit him."

The Cherokee laid his head back and closed his eyes in weariness. When Jess finished bandaging the wound, she returned to Mac's side. "Mac, are you all right?" she asked softly, watching his face.

He didn't reply as he worked to stop the bleeding, and she left to get more clean water.

Mac hardly heard Jessica's words, for the sounds and sights of that ghastly ambush still whirled in his head— the percussion of the musket fire echoing off the rocks, the sting in his shoulder, and the headlong crash into the ground when his horse fell. The next thing he remembered was seeing his companions who had also been struck down. In the fading light, he saw Tall Tree lying motionless in the dust. Oskati was crouching low, holding his arm and trying to spot the gunmen. Quiet Bear lay close by and Mac heard him moan. When he reached his old friend's side, Quiet Bear looked up at him, pain twisting the man's features as he gasped, "Why?"

With the light fading fast, Mac couldn't tell how serious Quiet Bear's wound was, but it was clear that his old friend was losing a lot of blood. Mac had been able to nearly stop the flow by packing it with cloth torn from his shirtsleeve. The ride back had seemed to take an eternity; Mac was amazed Quiet Bear had survived it. As they rode on and the initial shock wore off, Mac's anger grew. Stronger even than the anger, however, was the flood of guilt that overwhelmed him. It was his fault for suggesting the parley to start with. He should have known it was futile to try to reason with the land-hungry Whites. Now, taking a deep breath, he looked at Quiet Bear's face. The price of his naive optimism was too high, and he would never forgive himself for misjudging the situation.

On Jessica's way back to the bedroom, Gran appeared at the other doorway. "What is it, Jessica?" she asked, seeing the stricken look on Jess's face.

"They were ambushed on the way back. Quiet Bear is . . ." Gran followed her into the bedroom.

Jessica helped Mac bandage Quiet Bear's wound and left him resting as comfortably as possible, considering the severity of his injury. Mac and Oskati then carried Tall Tree's body to his house to await the burial service that would be held that evening. Oskati went home to rest.

Mac returned to the cabin, entered in silence, then sank wearily down on the deacon's bench next to the fireplace. One sleeve of his shirt had been torn away, having been used as bandaging for Quiet Bear. His forehead was slightly bruised from hitting his head as he fell when his horse had been hit by one of the musket balls meant for him. Mac had not appeared to be otherwise injured until Jess noticed the charred hole in his shirt at the top of his shoulder. Thankfully, it was only a minor wound, but his wife shuddered at the thought of her husband's close call.

Jess brought him a clean shirt and helped him into it. Then Gran handed him a second cup of coffee. Still he had not spoken. Finally, after finishing his coffee, Mac leaned his head back and closed his eyes.

"Mac, dear, you're exhausted. I'll bring you a blanket for the cot." Gran left the room to get the blanket, and Jessica sat down on the high-backed wooden bench next to him. He placed his arm wearily around her shoulders and pulled her close.

"I don't know how he held on 'til we made it home," he said quietly, laying his head against her soft hair. "He insisted we keep moving and get him back here."

"Mac, who could've done such a terrible thing?"

"It had to be the settlers. Riding fast, they could have easily circled around and reached the gap before us. No doubt they were afraid we'd bring help back to stop them."

"Did you talk with them?" she asked softly.

"Yes. They're coming here. They're desperate, Jess. That makes them much more dangerous. I never should have suggested trying to talk to them." His voice trailed away and he dozed off, giving in to his exhaustion.

Jessica remained beside him, his arm still about her. She placed her hand on his. His hands were strong, yet sensitive and talented enough to create wonderful patterns in silver and pewter. The thought that they would be taking up a weapon again in a fight caused her distress.

Jess knew Mac's anger was mostly directed at himself for suggesting the meeting in the first place. Her heart was pricked with the pain and guilt she knew he was feeling. Praying that he'd be able to realize he had done the right thing, she feared he would still feel responsible for the tragedy that had befallen them.

"Poor dear," Gran said as she returned to find him asleep. The two of them roused him and helped him make his way to the cot in the corner where he lay down and slept.

After checking on Quiet Bear, Jess walked onto the porch. She watched the sky brighten from gray to a soft saffron yellow just over the eastern ridges of the surrounding mountains. The thin mist shrouding the lower hills would soon burn away in the warmth of the morning sun.

Jess's mind was spinning. Shortly after noon today, most of the men would be returning from escorting their families to High Meadow. What would happen then? Jess knew that now Bear Paw and Mitakiah would be able to convince the others that attacking the settlers was justified.

Jess was uncertain about the Cherokee attitude toward revenge. She knew that many of the tribes had very strong blood-vengeance codes; it was one's absolute life-or-death duty to avenge the murder of a kinsman. This was one of the main reasons for so many of the clan wars among and within the eastern tribes.

Jess gripped the porch post in dread of what this day would bring and prayed, "Dear heavenly Father, the situation here seems so impossible. We need a miracle. Please give direction and wisdom to Mac and the others so no one else is hurt. And please, don't let Quiet Bear die."

The settlers' wagons would be entering the valley today but would not reach the village until at least tomorrow evening. With Quiet Bear lying gravely wounded and Tall Tree slain, only a miracle could prevent this lovely valley from becoming the sight of another bloody conflict.

Why had it come to this? The Iron Mountain settlement had been established for nearly forty years. The Indians had been a quiet, productive people. They had accepted the Christian religion brought to them by the elder Macklins and had dealt fairly and peacefully with the outside world of White colonists. When many of the Cherokee rose up against White encroachment, the people of Iron Mountain had avoided conflict. During the Revolutionary War they had kept a low profile and had not joined with those Cherokee declaring loyalty to the Crown in order to halt the flow of settlers along the frontier.

There was so much free land to be had. Why must these settlers have this particular land? How did they even know about it anyway? And what part did Little Sparrow and Howard Canfield play in all of this?

"Jessica," Gran came out of the house and touched her shoulder, "Quiet Bear is calling for you." Jess's heart sank as she looked into the older woman's sorrow-filled eyes. Swallowing the lump in her throat, she hurried to Quiet Bear's bedside. She knelt down beside the bed and gently touched his shoulder.

Quiet Bear opened his eyes. "Rea' na tani, you must not let River Walker seek to avenge me. There has to be another way. Our people will surely be destroyed. Promise me you'll make him find another way." Quiet Bear smiled weakly.

"But, Bear Paw will . . ."

"No." Quiet Bear coughed and hesitated a moment before he went on. "It's true he'll gladly use this as an excuse to claim blood vengeance. His bitterness and lack of respect for me is well known. It's River Walker I'm concerned about. If he seeks vengeance, the entire village will follow him. You must make him find another way."

Jess fought back hot tears. The request sounded next to impossible.

"Quiet Bear, please, just rest now . . . I'll go get Mac."

"No time," he gasped, clutching her hand. "Promise, Rea' na tani. . . . My pain is over, but the suffering of our people will just begin if he doesn't find a way to stop this thing."

"But—"

"Promise . . ." His strength was slipping away.

"I promise," she finally whispered, choking past her tears. "Somehow, we'll find a way."

Patting her hand gently, he smiled, "Now I can go home to heaven and see my Willow once more. Tell young River Walker that he has made his teacher very proud. I could not have been more proud of a son of my own flesh."

With that, Quiet Bear closed his eyes peacefully.

Jess stared at him. The now silent figure reminded her of the bronzed statue of a mighty Roman centurion Sir Gaston had kept in his library. Quiet Bear had been a strong and capable leader who was also sensitive to the needs of his people. In this moment, Jess couldn't really accept the fact he wouldn't be standing before the people at the Council meeting ever again.

"Oh, Lord, why him? Why now?" She gently moved his hand from hers to rest it across his chest. She wanted to call his name and wake him, but the painful realization it was over gripped her heart like a vise. "My poor darling Mac," she moaned to herself as she buried her face in her hands.

They did not awaken Mac immediately as there was nothing he could do, and he needed the rest to be prepared for whatever was to come. When he did wake up just before noon and learn about Quiet Bear, he sat beside his old friend and teacher's bed for a long time with his head bowed.

As he emerged, Jess could see the anger in her husband's eyes once more. His jaw was set grimly. Without a word to any of them, he quickly strode out the door.

"Mac—" Jess called.

"Better let him be, lass," Grandfather said sadly. "He'll need some time. Since our Andrew passed away, Quiet Bear has been like a father to him. It's a bitter thing to lose someone, but when it's like this . . ."

"Grandfather, I know he needs time," Jess said softly, choking back the lump in her throat. "But I made a promise to Quiet Bear that I must try to keep. From the look on Mac's face I can't wait. I must speak to him now."

She quickly followed her husband out the door and ran to catch up with his long strides.

"Mac darling, wait. Please. You must listen to me!" She clutched his arm and he stopped. His look was impatient. "Darling, I know you need time alone right now. I know how hurt and angry you are, but you must listen to me."

Jess related the promise she had made to Quiet Bear. "You must think of some way to stop the Cherokee from attacking."

"Stop them?" he declared icily through clenched teeth. "I'll lead them!"

"You can't mean that!" She refused to believe her ears.

Mac looked out over the valley. "Even if I didn't, no one can stop Bear Paw and Mitakiah from getting their way now."

"You must," she insisted.

He went on as though she hadn't spoken. "Quiet Bear taught me nearly everything I know about survival in the wild. He was my father's blood brother. During the war, he convinced the village people to remain neutral when the rest of the Cherokee, Creek, and Choctaw were declaring to fight for the Crown. He came himself to ride with the little band of rangers near Ellensgate when I was assigned to that area.

"Look how he's been repaid by the very people whose freedom he fought for. He was a good and wise man, Jess. He didn't deserve what they did to him."

"I know. I know," she agreed softly. "They should be punished for what they did. But only the guilty ones, not the innocent families. You can't lead men bent on vengeance in some wild attack. There'll be innocent children, men, and women hurt or even killed."

"They should have thought about that before they started this," he said flatly.

"Mac—" she gasped, clinging to his arm and suddenly feeling as though she were talking to a stranger. "I can't believe you're saying these things. You can't really mean you'd lead an attack on innocent families!"

"That's what they're intending to do if they don't get their way," he declared hotly and pried her fingers from his arm. "Jess, go on back."

"I won't, not until you listen to me!" she persisted in desperation, trying to think of something, anything, to divert his anger long enough for him to calm down. "Think about it, Mac. Something very strange is happening. Why have they come here? Why do they think they *can* come here? Something isn't right. To be here already, they had to leave Norfolk about the time Frye first talked to your grandparents. There's plenty of other land Frye and Canfield could have claimed. Why here? And another thing, what's Little Sparrow doing meeting secretly with Canfield? Take some time, please. Please think about it."

110

He looked at her a moment seemingly oblivious to her pleading. "What are you doing here, anyway?" he snapped. "You're supposed to be up at High Meadow with the other women and children."

"Your grandparents felt they should stay and I couldn't leave them alone," she replied, searching his face for some sign of recovered reason.

For a brief moment, the firmness in his jaw relaxed slightly. Then the determination returned, and he turned without another word and stormed angrily toward the village.

Jess's hands hung limply at her side in despair. This couldn't be happening! Their lovely dream of building a wonderful life together just couldn't be shattered by the deadly fury of revenge. For a moment she thought she had gotten through to him, but fury had engulfed him again.

Unable to bear the sight of him storming away, she closed her eyes and turned her head. Had she failed to keep her promise to Quiet Bear and lost Mac as well? Too distraught for tears, Jess turned back, opening her eyes to see the man for whom she would willingly give her life walk away as a stranger, bent on a terrible task of vengeance.

12

Upon returning to the cabin, Jess was on the verge of tears. She reluctantly explained her fears to Gran. Putting her arms around Jessica as she would a frightened child, Gran tried to calm her apprehension with repeated assurances that all would turn out all right.

"Perhaps," Jess wondered aloud, "just perhaps the settlers would listen to me and stop outside the valley."

"Jessica, my dear, you can't go to them," Gran replied gently, leaving no room for discussion. "It's much too dangerous. You must trust your husband to try to stop this from going any further. He has many friends in the village; they'll listen to him. You know what a good man he is, Jessica. He won't do what you fear. I just know it."

With all her heart Jessica wished she could share Gran's convictions, but Gran had not seen the fierce anger in Mac's eyes nor heard his bitter words. Touching her bracelet, she tried to erase the memory of his strong hand prying her fingers from his arm and the fury blazing in his eyes.

Shortly after the conversation with Gran, she was absently watching out the window when she caught sight of

Mac riding out alone. He was not leading a war party. A spark of hope leapt in her heart. Maybe he had come to his senses! Perhaps he was leaving to have a chance to think things through. She did not even want to consider the other possibility.

After leaving his wife on the path to the village, Mac had stormed to Oskati's house. With each of his steps her voice penetrated through the red haze of his fury. Jessica's questions were like irritating gnats interfering with his concentration on what must now be done.

As he was about to tap on his friend's door, he glanced back toward his grandparents' house and caught the glimpse of Jess disappearing inside. Why had he allowed her to come? He had said things she should never have had to hear him say. She would be in danger herself if the fighting reached the village. Why was she so stubborn? She hadn't even gone to High Meadow as he had insisted. Of course, she would never have left his grandparents alone. He could picture her wielding a musket, nearly as long as she was tall, in defense of them. The mental picture brought a smile to his lips; however, the smile faded quickly as he recalled their encounter a few moments ago. Would he ever be able to forget that frantic pleading in her voice or that fear of his anger in her eyes?

Oskati answered the door, and Mac entered still deeply in troubled thought.

"How is Quiet Bear?" Oskati asked.

Mac couldn't bring himself to say the words. He just shook his head gravely. Oskati drew in a breath and closed his eyes to shut out the awful news.

When Oskati looked at him again, Mac explained, "Quiet Bear spoke to Jessica just before he died. He made her promise to keep me from avenging his death and to find a way to stop this situation before it gets worse." Mac ran his hand through his dark hair in exasperation and began pacing. "It's an impossible request!" he insisted.

"Impossible," Oskati agreed strongly. "Even if we could put aside our desire for revenge—for justice—we could never convince the others to just stand back and let the settlers move in. I won't give up my home without a fight."

"Never!" Mac's anger permeated his entire being. Yet somehow Jess's pleading questions kept echoing in his ears. He could almost hear her voice. Then suddenly, the names of Little Sparrow and Canfield registered. What had she said? Little Sparrow secretly meeting with Frye's business partner?

"Oskati, Jess made a very strange comment just now." Mac momentarily stopped his angry pacing. "She asked about Little Sparrow and Howard Canfield being together. Do you know anything about that?"

Oskati thought a moment then shook his head. "Canfield first showed up here last spring not long after the wedding. In fact, I think he was here the week after you and Jess stayed at Sycamore Creek cabin for your honeymoon."

Mac considered this new bit of information and began pacing again. All at once, he stopped. The signature of Harold Smythe had come to mind. Harold Smythe was Sir Gaston's lawyer; he had been the executor of the will leaving the bulk of the Keene estate to Jess. A growing curiosity slowly edged against the raging anger within.

He felt somewhat relieved to have his intense emotions diverted a bit. He had never before experienced such a surge of savagery well up inside of him. He was shaken by the realization that he had wanted to destroy those responsible for his friend's death with his bare hands. Gradually, a measure of self-control returned. Mac couldn't help feeling that he had been drawn back from the brink of some terrible, dark abyss. He began to see that without Jessica's frantic persistence diverting his course, he could have plunged over the edge on a disastrous path from which there would have been no turning back.

Somewhere from the dim recesses of his memory came the words of his grandfather, "'Vengeance is mine, saith the Lord.' The Lord's retribution is sure and accurate, Mac."

"Mac, are you okay?" Oskati asked, pulling his friend out of deep thought. Mac leaned heavily against the window overlooking the valley. "Mac?" Oskati repeated.

"Oskati, what if it wasn't the settlers who ambushed us?"

"What?" the Cherokee asked in surprise. "Who else could it have been?"

"I don't know . . . I don't know, but I'm suddenly wondering about this whole thing. Jess may have been on to something. If only there was more time . . .

"Listen, the men will be coming back from High Meadow any time now. We won't be able to keep what's happened quiet for long. It'll take some time to prepare for the funeral service. The settlers can't reach us until tomorrow evening at the earliest. You must insist that nothing be done in retribution until after Quiet Bear and Tall Tree's funeral has been properly attended to."

"You're not going to be here?"

"I should make it back in time. But if I don't, I think Quiet Bear would understand and want me to try to carry out the promise Jess made."

Mac's heart began to pound as he spoke. "I'm going to take the trail up Jackson Falls and ride to Ellensgate to ask Harold Smythe some questions. He may have a clue about this whole thing. Using the back trail, I should be back before dark tonight."

Oskati still looked puzzled. "I don't know how it could possibly change anything. But if you think there's a chance, you must go. You do know, my friend, that I must also do what's necessary now, even if that means taking up arms against these intruders to protect my home."

The two young men looked each other squarely in the eye. Mac clasped his friend's hand in a firm grasp. "I would expect nothing less from you, Oskati. And if this is just a wild goose chase, I'll stand with you as soon as I return."

Within fifteen minutes, he was directing Ettinsmoor on the trail up toward Jackson Falls. Sir Gaston had reminded him of this shortcut out of the valley during the war. The trail was only accessible on horseback or foot and would only take a couple of hours.

Mac and Ettinsmoor zigzagged up the mountainside through a stand of young poplars and white-barked birches. The path was dappled with sunlight streaking down through yellow and red-orange leaves. Two crows reeled above the tops of the fir trees along the ridge, their raucous cawing echoing in the clear air. The trail climbed steeply beside a deep gash in the rocks. Many years before this had been the course of a tumbling waterfall escaping from a large spring near the top of Jackson Ridge. Now only a trickle of water seeped down the well-worn rocks.

Moving up the trail, Mac noticed that grass that had grown up along the path had been trampled down and had turned brown. This surprised him a little for it meant that someone had been using the trail. Because of the narrowness and difficulty of this path, it had never been used very much. Now, it appeared that the trail had been used at least two or three times fairly recently. It was possible that someone from the village was trading with the merchants at Ellensgate using this shortcut instead of the road through the gap. Still, it struck him as being odd.

Cresting the ridge, he could see rolling land stretching toward the east. Among the trees some ten miles due east, he could just make out a tiny cluster of buildings. These were the remains of the once elegant Keene estate owned by Sir Gaston Keene. Through the trees five miles off to the south, he could see the spire of the little church at Ellensgate. Another hour of riding time would bring him to the law office of Harold Smythe and perhaps some answers to the questions Jess had posed.

13

Many of the southeastern tribes had very specific traditions when it came to preparing for war. These often included three days of fasting and then a feast before the attack. Councils of war were held to recruit volunteers for the battle with the women singing war chants to encourage their men to brave exploits.

The situation facing the people at Iron Mountain, however, was unique. Over the years these people had accepted many of the White ways, including Christianity. Because of this, they had laid aside some of their old traditions. Yet they weren't a people who would lie down and meekly turn over their homes to intruders. With the settlers on their doorstep, there was no time for fasting or old rituals anyway. The villagers also faced the sad duty of caring and showing proper respect for their fallen leaders. This dilemma caused a dismal cloud of fatalistic uncertainty to descend upon the village. The people couldn't be sure of what would happen now; however, considering what had been the most common outcome of other such conflicts over the land, the Cherokee people had little hope of a happy ending for them.

From the Macklins' porch, Jess could hear shouts and mournful wailing as the men received the dreadful news. As she listened to the distressing din, she prayed for Mac's safety and wondered where he might be.

Soon four young men came to the house to carry Quiet Bear's body away to be prepared for burial. Grandfather Macklin spoke briefly with them as they carried out their solemn duty. He would perform the funeral service at dusk.

Throughout the afternoon Oskati was busy talking with the men in meetings trying to decide what must be done. He convinced them to wait until Quiet Bear and Tall Tree had been properly honored. Beyond this, however, little had been decided. Bear Paw and his followers were also making their influence felt. Many who had been undecided before were now listening more attentively to Bear Paw's outrage, and the Indian was becoming more vocal as the afternoon dragged on.

Many of the younger men had never known anything but the peaceful life they had enjoyed. Some of the older ones remembered the past of clan wars and territorial fights before the Macklins. They had no desire to return to those times. Still others, young and old, had become restless with their gentle, uneventful way of life. These men longed for the days of old glory, of proving one's manhood in battle. They were especially receptive to Bear Paw's comments.

As the hours passed, Jess became more and more uneasy about Mac. When it approached time for the services, she went down to the village to tell the young men that Grandfather was ready to be carried to the meetinghouse. After doing this, she passed the stables only to hear her name called in a hoarse whisper. She looked around but saw no one near. Puzzled, Jess stepped forward then heard her name again. She turned and saw the shadowed form of a young Cherokee just inside the doorway of the stable.

"Mrs. Macklin," he said quietly. "Please come here. It's your husband. He's hurt and needs you."

A heart-wrenching fear swept through her. Jess quickly entered the stable door. "What's happened? Where is he?"

While she had seen this man in the village before, she was not acquainted with him. But the urgency in his voice and grave look on his face turned any apprehension she may have had for herself into fear for Mac.

"Come, I'll take you to him. We must go the back way though. Everyone's upset enough as it is. That's why you must come alone."

"Let me get my horse," she said, following him out the back.

"That's been taken care of. I've already saddled one for you."

If she had been thinking more clearly, she would have asked more questions, but all she could think about was Mac's being hurt and needing her. Nothing else mattered but reaching his side.

The two of them mounted the waiting horses and rode off into the late afternoon sunlight. Dusk would soon fall, but Jess hardly noticed. She was concentrating on only one thing—getting to Mac as quickly as possible.

They rode northward at a furious pace. A small bay mare whose black mane and tail whipped wildly in the wind carried Jess. Sensing the urgency in her rider's gentle hand, the horse stretched her stride to its maximum.

While the young brave's horse was quick, he couldn't match the speed of Jess's mount, and Jess had to hold her back every once in a while when she pulled ahead.

They had nearly covered the length of the valley when the light faded to a misty gloom. Jess recognized the trail. "Is he at the Sycamore Creek cabin?" she called to the Indian.

"Yes." The answer came above the sound of pounding hooves. "We're almost there."

As the path edged upward into the tree-lined slope, Jess knew the way very well. This was the cabin where she and Mac had spent their honeymoon five months earlier.

She remembered how lovely the spring had been. Perhaps everything seemed more wonderful then. The cool spring nights had been filled with the warmth of their long-anticipated passion. Sparkling days of sunshine, love, and laughter had followed. Nearly every day they had strolled along the path, arm in arm, enjoying the glorious spring days in the picturesque setting. They had relished that precious slice of time together without the stress of the past two difficult years and the war.

During those walks, they had talked about their dreams for the future and shared important things from their past. They had laughed and even sung a few little Scottish tunes each had learned as a child. Mac had fascinated her with stories of Indian legends, and he had taught her new things about the forest. Each day she had gathered wild purple-fringed orchids and yellow buttercups or crested dwarf irises and fairy wand along the way and had taken them back to the cabin to decorate their table.

The days and nights had passed quickly. When the week was over they both were reluctant to leave the lovely hideaway. Mac had promised to bring her back again. She never dreamed it would be under such dreadful circumstances.

Her attention was quickly brought to the present when she saw the cabin. The place was dark. They approached it and dismounted. Jess ran up the stone steps to the rough-hewn door. Her Cherokee guide got there first.

Jess didn't notice the new heavy latch on the outside of the door frame. Her heart pounded with apprehension as the young man pushed open the heavy door. Stepping through the doorway, Jess peered inside.

Instantly, a rough hand grabbed her wrist, wrenching her bracelet away. Stunned, she turned and reached for the young brave's hand, but he pushed her back, sending her reeling into the darkness. A loud, solid bang sounded as the door slammed shut behind her.

The cabin was pitch black. Catching herself on the table, Jess kept from falling and groped back toward the door. Pulling against it, she screamed, "What are you doing? What's going on? Where's Mac?"

"I'm just a messenger, lady. I wouldn't know." The rasping sound of the new wooden latch sliding into place told her that the door had been barred from the outside. Jess yanked on it anyway, then she kicked the door. Why had she been such a fool? And now what was she going to do?

14

Mac had been in Harold Smythe's office once before, on the day Sir Gaston's will had been read. Jessica had come to Smythe trying to learn the reason Sir Gaston had left the bulk of his estate to her instead of his grandson, Gregory. Smythe told her that Sir Gaston had discovered that Gregory had betrayed Mac to the Tory and British soldiers, resulting in a trap being set for Mac at the Keene estate. Smythe felt that Gaston might have been able to forgive his grandson for siding with the Tories out of loyalty to the Crown. However, the old patriot could not interpret Gregory's support as anything other than treachery because it had been for opportunistic reasons. Gregory had never imagined that the "rag-tag" Continental army led by George Washington would ever be able to defeat the most powerful nation in the world. He was only concerned with preserving his inheritance, the Keene estate, so he could eventually return to Austria.

Smythe's office looked out onto the main street of Ellensgate. It was small and neat except for the desk, behind which the attorney sat. A portly man in his late fifties, Smythe dressed conservatively in a black frock coat, breeches, and a stiffly starched white shirt influenced by his Puritan background. Although appearing solemnly formal, he had a twinkle in his eyes that he allowed very few people to see. Mac and Jessica had become members of that select group shortly after their first meeting.

Smythe's pleasant mood at seeing Mac for the first time since the wedding soon became sober. Mac began asking questions about the attorney's involvement in the sale of the land at the Iron Mountain mission through Carlson Frye.

"Why yes, Mac, I remember the sale. I was very sorry to hear that your grandfather's poor health had forced them to close the mission. And I was rather surprised to hear that most of the Cherokee were moving farther west. I thought old Quiet Bear would never leave that valley."

"He won't," Mac said grimly, and he related the tragic events of the previous night.

"I can't believe it." Smythe was stunned. "Frye had letters from the Assembly. He was helping a party of folks after they'd been burned out of their homes and that seemed very admirable. And, of course, he had that letter from your grandfather."

"What letter?" Mac asked.

"The letter signing over his power of attorney to Carlson Frye to dispose of the property in a fair and equitable manner," Smythe answered as he recalled each detail.

"My grandfather never signed any such paper!" Mac said, trying to control his anger.

Smythe could hardly believe that he had been duped into helping in a fraudulent land steal. He lamented, "You'd think an old codger like me would have seen through such deception. Granted, I've never seen your grandfather's signature, but I had no reason to believe anyone wished him harm or would ever try such an unscrupulous plot to get the mission land.

"Who would've ever thought anyone other than locals even knew about that valley and the mission. Hardly anyone from the village comes over here to Ellensgate. It's much easier to get to Jasper through the gap up toward the north end of the valley, not that they travel much that way either since they seem pretty self-sufficient up there."

"Wait a minute," Mac interrupted. "You say hardly anyone comes over here from the village?"

"That's right. Why I can't remember the last time old Tall Tree's son brought him over the Jackson Falls trail for some of the peppermint sticks the old fellow used to love."

"Well, someone has been using that trail, and very recently!" Mac exclaimed.

His frustration with the number of unanswered questions was increasing. He could see Smythe shared this frustration. The older gentleman threw his pen on his desk, stood up, and began pacing back and forth. "Maybe it's the ghosts from the old Keene estate," Smythe speculated.

"Ghosts?"

Mac's question stopped Smythe long enough for the attorney to wave his hand to negate his previous comment as not serious. But Mac was ready to grasp at any bit of information that might give him a clue about what was happening.

"Oh, it's nothing . . . nothing really," Smythe answered. "It's just that for the past few months several people traveling out that way at night have reported seeing a light coming from over by the ruins of the Keene mansion. Since only the main house burned down that awful night you and Jessica were nearly killed and Bradford and Gregory died, I'm sure some weary stranger traveling through just stopped to find shelter for the night in the stables or the field hands' house."

Mac was inclined to agree, but that still didn't explain who had been using the Jackson Falls trail. Then Smythe added thoughtfully, "You know there is one curious thing, though. You mentioned a fellow named Canfield was with Carlson Frye? Now, I never saw those two together, but a man named Howard Canfield came to my office last May claiming to be Bradford Keene's brother from England. He was inquiring into whatever might be left of Bradford's estate. When I told him it had all been confiscated by the Continental army, he took the news amazingly well.

"This Canfield fella wanted to know how to locate Jessica. It was just after your wedding come to think of it. He said there'd been quite a commotion stirred up in Cheltenham when the news came out about the Keene family jewel collection being returned to the museum there. He wanted to express his admiration for her generous decision . . . Which reminds me, your coming here today is quite a coincidence."

"Coincidence?" Mac asked, only half-listening. The pieces of this very strange puzzle still did not fit.

"Yes. There are two more strangers who've come to town looking for Jessica."

Now Smythe had Mac's full attention. "They're representatives from the Cheltenham Museum who've come in person to get Jessica's signature on the papers signing ownership of the jewels to the museum. I was getting everything in order to travel with the gentlemen over to Dunston to see you young folks. One is a security agent, a big fellow, and the other is the nephew of the museum director."

Just then a knock at the door interrupted their conversation, and the door opened.

"Ahh, Mr. Hampton and Mr. Melden, please come in. I was just talking about you."

The sun was settling below the western crest of hills as Mac made his way back along the Jackson Falls trail. His discussion with Harold Smythe had answered some of his questions but had raised others that were even more disturbing.

To add to his frustration, Mac now found himself saddled with the two Englishmen. After a brief discussion in Smythe's office, they had invited themselves along. The younger one would have been more than happy to wait at Ellensgate until Mac could bring Jessica by Smythe's office, but the older one had insisted they accompany Mac and see Jessica without delay.

Mac had countered that now was not a good time to be visiting Iron Mountain and he had left Smythe's office, but the two men had followed him. Short of threatening them with bodily harm, he warned them he was in a hurry and would not wait for them along the trail. If they got lost, it would be their own fault.

While at Smythe's office Mac had been surprised to learn there had been three Keene brothers: Sir Gaston, Lord John, Sir Thompson, and a sister, Lady Cecilly Keene-Canfield. Sir Thompson had died before the other brothers came to the colonies; his widow remarried and bore two sons, Howard and Bradford. When the boys were eight and nine years old, their mother and father were lost at sea crossing the English Channel on their way to the Continent. Howard was taken in by Lord John's sister, Lady Cecilly, and Bradford was adopted by Lord John and his wife.

Samuel Hampton had unwittingly increased Mac's uneasiness by describing Howard Canfield as a notoriously ruthless businessman with few scruples. Mac remembered Bradford Keene's unprincipled ruthlessness, which had included a plot to murder Jessica for her inheritance from Sir Gaston. He shuddered to think that the ordeal begun at Ellensgate nearly two years ago might not really be over.

Smythe's parting remark further added to Mac's anxiety. He had related that Oscar Stinson, one of Bradford's accomplices in the former attempt on Jessica's life, had disappeared while waiting to hang for the murder of two influential plantation owners during the war.

Stinson! That's who that was! Now Mac realized what was familiar about that man with Tobias Alder riding as scout at the settlers' camp.

Mac only had an isolated fact here and a strange coincidence there, but taken together the pieces were beginning to fit like a strange jigsaw puzzle—a very disturbing puzzle.

Mac would have liked to press Ettinsmoor, but he allowed the big stallion to pick his way carefully back down the zig-zagging trail. It was an agonizing descent.

"Mr. Macklin, are you sure this is a proper trail?" Hampton called, clinging to the saddle for dear life.

Mac wasn't listening. His mind was whirling with the information he had just learned. He had found out enough to suspect that the land deal was covering something more sinister. The fact that Howard Canfield was Bradford Keene's brother and was teamed up with Oscar

Stinson in a landgrab scheme was bad enough. However, the idea that he had appeared at Iron Mountain after looking for Jessica at Smythe's office caused a tight knot of anxiety to grow deep inside of Mac.

"Ohhh!"

Mac turned quickly to see Hampton crashing to the ground, saddle and all, his cry still echoing along the rocky chasm beside the trail. The young man's horse trotted nervously forward, edging into Ettinsmoor. Mac grabbed the riderless horse's headstall.

"What happened, Hampton?" he asked impatiently as Samuel struggled to disentangle himself from the stirrups and saddle.

"The blasted cinch broke. I could've been killed," he spluttered with outrage, trying to cover up his embarrassment.

Mac noticed Melden shaking his head derisively. While his own patience was wearing thin, Mac could see the strained relationship between the two Englishmen. It was obvious that the older one was far superior in agility, strength, and size. It was also evident he didn't try to hide his intolerance of the younger one's ineptness. Mac couldn't help but feel a bit sorry for the lad; he had never cared for people lording their abilities over others less gifted.

However, he really had no time for these delays. He must get back before a terrible mistake was made. He must get back to Jess.

Dismounting quickly, Mac led Hampton's horse back to him. "You'll have to ride bareback," he said gruffly.

"But, I can't . . . I mean, I won't," Hampton said as he dusted himself off, apparently trying to regain some shred of dignity.

"Then you'll have to walk back or stay here until another saddle can be brought up. Whichever you decide, I have to be on my way." Mac's patience was at an end. He couldn't stand here any longer wasting precious time listening to a spoiled tenderfoot.

The young man quickly looked away, trying to hide his reaction. Over the past few months, he had learned to pay little attention to Melden's comments. Surprisingly enough, however, this American's opinion mattered to him. Hampton had watched Mac in Smythe's office and had been impressed by his inner strength. Mac was confident without being self-satisfied like Melden. Although not that much older in years than Hampton, this American had a maturity about him, perhaps born on the battlefield during the Revolutionary War. After all that Smythe had already told them about Andrew Macklin, Hampton had come to the quick conclusion that Macklin was the kind of man someone could look up to, the kind of man he'd like to be someday.

Catching a glimpse of the hurt, Mac recovered his composure. He realized the young man's bluster was an attempt to hide his insecurity. Sighing, he said, "Listen, it's not difficult. You can do it. Many Indians prefer to ride without a saddle. Come on, I'll give you a lift up."

Hampton assumed his self-confident air and tried to appear nonchalant. "Very well, I suppose it would be more comfortable than walking all the way." He hesitated then stepped on Mac's interlocked hands and swung up on the horse's back. Clutching nervously at the tuft of mane at the horse's withers, Hampton gripped the horse as tightly as he could with his legs and tried to appear at ease as he took the reins.

130

The delay had only taken minutes, but to Mac it seemed like hours. He was relieved to hear nothing more from Hampton. Even if he had, he wasn't going to waste any more time listening to it. He had too many other things on his mind now.

His immediate concern was trying to convince the Cherokee to investigate the situation before running off on a tirade of revenge. But that problem worried him less right now than the thought of Jessica being unaware of possible danger. She had no way of knowing that Howard Canfield was anything other than a land speculator. Knowing how Little Sparrow felt about Jess, the mental picture of Howard Canfield and the Indian girl together increased Mac's anxiety for his young bride.

He tried to reassure himself that Oskati and his other friends would see to it that she was safe. Still he couldn't shake the growing anxiety that if someone had really devised an elaborate plot, they may have planned an effective way to get to Jessica.

The pace along the mountain trail seemed painfully, ploddingly slow. Adding to Mac's misery was the memory of his last angry words to Jess. Filled with regret, he groaned inwardly, "Jess, why'd I ever let you come here?"

By the time they reached the village, darkness had settled over the valley like a dense black blanket. Far off to the north sporadic flashes of faint light appeared in the clouds. The air hung heavy and still, ominous evidence of an approaching storm moving in over the northwestern ridge.

Noticing the distant flashes, Mac was reminded of a similar scene a year and a half earlier while he lay badly wounded in a field hospital. However, the lights in those clouds had been caused by cannon fire. That night he had

131

felt frustration at not being able to fulfill his duties, especially since the tide of the war seemed at last to favor the Continental army. But Mac was able to fulfill his duties tonight. He wasn't wounded, and his first duty was to find Jess. Then he must do what he could to honor her promise to Quiet Bear.

The sound of low, mournful hymn singing brought Mac back to the present. He realized they were probably on the very brink of another battle—a battle in the undeclared war that had been waging between those settlers wanting to expand their boundaries and the Indians who resisted the intrusion into their lands.

By the time the three men had ridden to the stables and taken care of their horses, the crowd at the little cemetery was winding its way back down the hill behind the meetinghouse. Mac and the two Englishmen reached the oak tree at the center of the village green about the same time as the mourners. Bear Paw, who had worked his way to the front of the procession, turned with a small lantern held high. Motioning for the people to stop and listen, he did not see Mac.

"My people, we have paid our respects to our leaders as Oskati has asked. Now we must bring out our drums and begin to dance, to prepare ourselves for the justice we must bring upon the treacherous dogs who have taken the lives of our two great leaders."

Bear Paw's timing had been flawless. He had caught the people at a painfully emotional pitch, very vulnerable to suggestions for seeking revenge. Mac heard the words and saw the grim faces of the crowd touched by the lantern light. Most were nodding their heads in agreement.

Quietly he told Hampton and Melden to remain back in the shadows, out of sight.

"Bear Paw, I'm sure your uncle would be touched by your sudden deep regard for him now that he's gone . . . Very surprised at your change of opinion of him as well, no doubt."

The Indian turned quickly at the unexpected sound of Mac's voice, but rather than falter, the agitator smiled with the calm assurance of his superior position.

"River Walker! We've been wondering about you. I thought perhaps you had chosen to avenge my uncle yourself. Or perhaps you felt too guilty for leading Quiet Bear and Tall Tree into a death trap to show yourself at their funeral."

With a reflex action Mac swung a lightning quick uppercut that connected with Bear Paw's jawbone and sent him reeling backwards against Mitakiah, who had been right behind. Bear Paw was caught off guard by the quickness and strength of the blow. As Mitakiah helped steady him on his feet, the two exchanged glances of satisfaction.

Catching this, Mac immediately realized he had played right into their hands. So be it, he thought.

Mac had surprised himself by his reaction. He realized the comment about feeling guilty had struck a nerve. However, that was only a part of it. The clash between him and Bear Paw had been building for a long time. Although his knuckles still smarted, Mac couldn't deny his feeling of satisfaction for having finally done what he had so often been tempted to do in the past.

Quiet Bear's nephew had always resented the close friendship between Quiet Bear and Mac's father and the obvious pride the two men had taken in the accomplishments Mac achieved while growing up. Over the years Bear Paw had belittled and tried to embarrass his uncle. Out of respect for Quiet Bear, Mac had restrained himself from challenging the young man before. As head of the village Council, Quiet Bear had managed to control the situation and keep his unruly nephew in check.

Although this would not have been Mac's choice of time or place, he could not back down if he were to have any further influence with the people. While he had never tried to play a leading role in village affairs up to now, he was aware that his opinion was valued. Aside from his personal dislike for Bear Paw, the fact that circumstances surrounding his wife might be behind the present crisis facing the village meant it was up to him to prevent the impending catastrophe, even if that meant a deadly confrontation with Bear Paw.

A glint of steel flashed in the uneven light of the lantern as the Indian brave raised a wickedly sharp knife. The crowd of men moved back to allow room for the fight, when suddenly James Macklin pushed through the crowd and stepped in front of Bear Paw.

"How dare you dishonor your uncle by this impudence!"

"Will River Walker hide behind his ailing grandfather?" taunted Bear Paw.

"Grandfather, step aside," Mac warned steadily. "There's no avoiding this. Take Gran and Jess into the meetinghouse and keep them there." Mac's steady gaze never wavered from his opponent's face.

"Andrew, I forbid this! We can't be fighting among ourselves now . . ." The old gentleman stepped unsteadily toward his grandson, and Mac caught him by the arm.

"Oskati," Mac called to his friend who had already stepped forward. "Take him and Gran and Jess inside."

Gran supported one arm while Oskati supported the other. Mac looked quickly for Jessica but she was not there.

134

"Jess?" Mac called, suddenly gripped with a desperate need to see his wife's face appear in the crowd.

"Wasn't she with you during the service, Oskati?" Gran asked, suddenly aware that she hadn't spoken with Jess for quite some time.

"She wasn't with me," Oskati replied.

"Perhaps she went to see about Little Sparrow," Gran was growing more uneasy. "Little Sparrow didn't go with the others to High Meadow yesterday either."

Mac was now totally distracted from the impending fight. "Has anyone seen Jessica or Little Sparrow?"

The crowd stirred, questioning each other, and Bear Paw pushed angrily forward.

"What's the matter now?" The Indian brandished his weapon menacingly. "Does River Walker have a change of heart? He seems to forget we have unfinished business here."

A distant rumble of thunder was accompanied by a fresh gust of wind across the green. The dry leaves rustled overhead.

"We'll finish our business as soon as I know my wife is safe," Mac said, leaving no room for further discussion.

At precisely that moment, the sound of rapid hoofbeats approached along the street coming up from the valley. A single horse and rider jolted to a halt at the edge of the green, and the rider slid to the ground. Running toward the crowd, he stopped before Mac. He was so out of breath, he couldn't speak so he held out a small object. Mac recognized it instantly just by the feel of it—Jess's bracelet.

"Where'd you get this, Coyote?" he asked, grabbing the young man's shoulder.

"She . . . she gave it to me. She said to give it to you and tell you to . . . to bring help." Coyote gasped, still breathless.

"Where is she?" Mac demanded.

Coyote cringed, then swallowed hard. "The . . . the settlers have her."

Angry grumbling surged through the crowd.

"How? Why?" Mac was stunned by this revelation as it did not fit at all with the picture he had begun to develop.

Coyote went on. "She thought she could convince them to turn back, so she asked me to take her to their camp. They wouldn't listen. They took us captive, but I was able to get away. She told me to give you this and to bring back as many men as possible to rescue her because the settlers mean to fight."

Mac clutched the bracelet tightly and clenched his teeth in anger.

Gran stepped forward. "Oh dear. She did mention doing just that earlier today. Mac, what are you going to do?"

Mac's mind reeled with anguish at the thought of his precious Jessica in the clutches of the treacherous settlers. Tobias Alder was a frightened, desperate man. Desperate, yes, but treacherous? A kidnapper? But then there was Oscar Stinson, and Mac knew that he was capable of anything.

If only Mac had listened to her, or at least let her know what he was doing, maybe she wouldn't have gone off on her own. As stubborn as Jess was, Mac knew she'd do nearly anything to keep her promise and prevent the fighting. Wait a minute, he thought as he looked at the bracelet in his hand. Was it reasonable to think Jess would ask a band of enraged, vengeance-seeking men to come to her rescue? Not his Jess. Not when she was so intent on keeping the two factions apart.

Thunder rumbled again in the distance. Mac started to ask Coyote another question when he caught a quick nod passing between Coyote and Bear Paw. Suddenly a warning signal blared inside.

Mustering every ounce of self-control, Mac grabbed the young Cherokee's shoulder. "Coyote will come with me and draw a map of the settlers' camp. With this storm moving in, we won't be able to do anything tonight. We'll ride in the morning."

Mac turned to Oskati. "Will you see about Gran and Grandfather for me? I want Coyote to fill me in on all the details while it's fresh on his mind."

Oskati nodded, "I'll bring them right along."

"Come on, Coyote," Mac directed with authority. "You can tell me the whole thing."

Coyote looked nervously back at Bear Paw. Mac kept a vise-like grip on his shoulder.

"You know, Coyote, I find it a little surprising that my wife asked *you* to take her to the settlers. I didn't know you two had met."

Hampton and Melden emerged from the shadows, extremely interested by what was happening. "We should have gotten her signature a month ago," Melden lamented as if it were Hampton's fault. "Now, we may be too late."

Hampton looked at him with true disgust. That comment didn't deserve any discussion. The young Englishman left his colleague behind to follow Mac and the young Cherokee to the Macklins' cabin.

Coyote did not know what to do. Perhaps he shouldn't have been so willing to be involved in this plot. But he needn't worry, he assured himself, all he had to do was stick to his story. He could guess what Bear Paw would do to him if he told the truth. He had to hold to his story.

A vivid picture crossed the young man's mind. Out on the western hills of the valley, he had happened once upon a young coyote attacking a bald eagle with an injured wing. Another huge eagle had swooped from the sky, snatched the skinny coyote in its sharp talons, and dropped it over a high rocky ledge. That day Coyote had learned a lesson: An eagle will ferociously protect its mate.

The Indian brave felt uncomfortably like a skinny coyote about to be dropped over a rocky ledge.

15

Once Jessica faced the fact she had been locked in, she began groping for a small clay lamp of bear oil kept on the mantel along with a tinderbox and flint striker. She could smell the strong odor of the oil. Thankful to find an adequate amount of it, she felt around for the short piece of milkweed wick still curled inside. Finally a tiny flame spluttered, then danced hungrily on the tip of the wick. In the thick darkness, this tiny light helped.

Holding her hand to shield the flame, she walked a quick round of the small cabin. She was truly alone, and she prayed that the rest of what the young Indian had told her about Mac was also untrue.

Going from window to window, she checked the shutters to see if they might have been left unlatched. They were all tightly secured from the outside. Jess sat down at the table trying to make some sense of the situation.

What reason would anyone have for wanting her locked away? She gently touched the stinging abrasion on her wrist. Why would someone do such a thing? Jess wondered if Little Sparrow could be behind this. She remembered the look in Little Sparrow's eyes when the girl first caught sight of Jessica's bracelet. Adá had warned her Little Sparrow was vindictive. Was this her doing?

By this time, Grandmother and Grandfather Macklin would surely be wondering about her. There may even be a search party, but how would they know where to begin? Maybe she hadn't even been missed! With all of the problems at the village, no one may have even realized she was gone. Gran knew Jess was going to call the young men to carry Grandfather to the meetinghouse. They might think she'd just gone ahead to talk to Oskati about Mac.

With the sun down, the evening air had grown quite cool. Since the day had been so warm, Jess had not carried her shawl to the village. Now she wished she had. There was no wood for the fireplace so she could do nothing to chase away the chill.

Pacing nervously, she tried to think about what she should do. Thoughts of a similar predicament a year and a half before surfaced in her mind. She and Mac had been abducted by Bradford Keene and his accomplices. They had planned a fatal carriage accident to remove her as heiress to the bulk of Sir Gaston's large estate. Bradford Keene, an avowed Loyalist, also sought revenge against Mac for his activities as an American agent. Robbie had been kidnapped, too, and all of them left in a deserted carriage house, bound and gagged. Mac had managed to use a piece of broken glass to cut the cords binding his wrists and then set the other two free. But Mac had been with her then. He had no idea where she was now. What if he really was hurt or being held captive somewhere else?

She tried to push these unpleasant speculations from her mind and concentrate on something more useful. Glancing about the room, she was filled with pleasant memories of the place. "Mac, my dearest, where are you?" she whispered, fighting the mounting panic.

"All right, Jessica Macklin, just stop it now!" she reprimanded herself. "There has to be a way out of here just like there was from the carriage house."

Jess walked to the windows again. Since the heavy shutters were barred from the outside, she knew the leather hinges could be cut if only she had a knife. She searched the tiny cupboard but found that all of the eating utensils had been removed. The plates were pewter, and Jess wished they had been china or pottery so she could break one into sharp pieces. The clay oil lamp could be broken, but she knew from experience that the oil saturated clay would just crumble without leaving any true edges.

Someone had been very thorough in removing anything that would aid an escape. The chairs, table, bed, and tiny cupboard were the only furnishings left. Even the hatchet had been taken from the wood box.

Not wanting to admit defeat, Jess sighed in frustration and sat down. She laid her head on her folded arms on the table to rest a minute. Sleepless nights and the stressful situation at the village had been very taxing. She was engulfed by an overwhelming tide of helplessness. Biting her lip, she fought back threatening tears, determined not to give in to hysteria.

Suddenly, she bolted up. The chairs! Perhaps she could use one of the chairs to batter at the shutters. Anything was better than sitting idle and letting herself sink into despair.

The chairs had been built of chestnut limb sections, smoothed down with a drawknife and joined together with wet rawhide thongs, which, when dried, shrunk to a taut, strong bond. The seat was also a wide section of leather, probably buffalo hide. It had been stretched taut, too.

Although the chairs were heavy, Jess managed to pick one up. Raising it high enough to smash against the chest high windows, however, was another matter. Jess let it fall back to the floor with a loud, solid thud. It was too heavy to raise and swing enough times to do the job.

Sinking back down in the chair, Jess felt an empty gnawing in her stomach. She had been too distraught over Quiet Bear's death and Mac's angry reaction to eat at noon. Thinking about the warm huckleberry and maize bread with fresh butter and cold buttermilk, thin slices of venison backstrap, and sweet potatoes to be served after the funeral service made the hunger even more intense. She closed her eyes and leaned her head back against the wall, trying not to think about it.

Finally dozing a bit, she awoke with a start. Having no idea what time it was, Jess was unable to guess how long she had been there. She didn't think she had slept long, so it probably was not yet midnight.

The deep-throated rumble of thunder in the distance made her realize what had awakened her. The warm air from the valley floor was rising to meet the cooler air coming down from the north. The result would undoubtedly be rain before too much later this night. The thunder seemed to set an ominous mood, and a shiver traveled up her spine.

Another noise caught her attention. It was outside. Jess stepped over and pressed her ear against the door. Voices!

With bated breath, she backed away to stand by the table to meet whomever would be coming through the door.

The scraping noise of someone lifting the heavy latch sounded. With a pounding heart, Jess prayed, "Please be Mac."

The heavy door creaked as it slowly swung open. Footsteps came forward. Jessica's heart sank. Stepping into the dim glow of the tiny lamp was Howard Canfield.

"Well, well, Jessica Macklin. Isn't this a pleasant surprise!"

"Canfield," she said, trying to catch her breath and control the waver in her voice. "What's all this about?"

"My, it's dismal in here." Turning to speak into the dark shadows behind him, he added, "Sparrow, dear, please get a couple of those tallow candles in the satchel on the buggy while I keep an eye on our guest."

"Little Sparrow is with you?"

"Yes. She's deliciously devious but really quite lovely, don't you think?" In the dimness his wickedly smug smile struck a deep chord of fear within her. She felt as if she was reliving a nightmare, only she was in this bad dream by herself.

In a moment Little Sparrow appeared at the door. With a decidedly superior air, she tilted a tallow candle to the tiny flame of the oil lamp. The new wick caught, and she placed it on the table in a small wooden holder.

"Ahhh, that's better," Canfield smiled. "Do light the other one, too."

Little Sparrow looked at him in cold silence as she lighted the other candle and placed it on the table next to the one already aglow.

"Now then," Canfield turned to Jessica and looked almost apologetic. "I must say we hadn't intended to do this. If Oscar and his friends hadn't been so clumsy in their ambush—missing Oskati and your husband—this

143

wouldn't have been necessary. It would have been far less complicated."

"Oscar?" Jess tried to remember where she had heard that name before.

"Oscar Stinson, one of my brother's right-hand men. You know my brother, Bradford Keene." Canfield's voice took on a sinister tone. "I believe you've met Oscar before, haven't you? He and his friend, Johnson, are outside."

Jessica's knees nearly buckled, and she leaned back against the table, unable to believe what she was hearing.

"Bradford? You're Bradford Keene's brother?" she stammered.

"Of course." An almost ghoulish smile crept across his lips. "Perhaps you didn't know. Our parents were lost in the Channel when we were quite young. Dear Uncle John adopted Bradford; Aunt Cecilly adopted me. I've been here in the colonies—excuse me, the States—to check into Bradford's estate."

She steeled herself before she asked the next question. "But what does that have to do with Fair View Land Company and us?"

"Everything, my dear. Everything." He looked toward the Indian woman who was standing beside the table like a statue. "Little Sparrow actually gave me the brilliant inspiration for this plan. Until I met her last spring, I wasn't sure how I was going to accomplish gaining the Keene jewel collection.

"When Smythe told me you had sold the stocks in Uncle Gaston's shipbuilding companies and given half to your new Congress, I knew I wouldn't be able to touch them, but when I found out you had generously endowed the museum with the collection of jewels, I could hardly

144

believe it. I couldn't imagine anyone being so utterly foolish or so utterly altruistic, I'm not sure which.

"At first I thought I'd go to Vienna and intercept the transfer documents. Then I learned that a security agent and museum representative were coming from England in person to obtain your signature. That meant the only way for me to stop the endowment and gain the jewels was to have you meet an untimely end before signing them over.

"You see, I've made a few unwise investments lately and without the jewels, I'm at the point of financial ruin. Several of my creditors have a nasty habit of collecting in blood what they cannot in money. Can you understand? This has all been necessary, my dear."

"I still don't see how that has anything to do with the Fair View Land Company," Jess insisted.

Canfield studied her a moment and rubbed his chin thoughtfully. "You know, it really is such a wonderfully complicated scheme, it seems a shame not to tell you about it. What could it hurt? I mean, when it's all over you won't be around to tell anyone."

Jessica was still recovering from the shock of learning that Canfield was Bradford Keene's brother. Sinking back in her chair, she listened in numb silence as the Englishman told her how he had come to Iron Mountain to meet her and discover a way to accomplish his task. Unfortunately, he arrived a day too late. Jess and Mac had already returned to Dunston after their honeymoon. He met Little Sparrow and in their mutual desire to hasten Jessica's demise, they had hit upon the idea of a volatile conflict between the westward-moving settlers and the Indians. The idea was so far-fetched, no one would ever suspect foul play. It had been a simple thing to enlist Little Sparrow's brother, Bear Paw, and friends to begin agitating bitter feelings among the Cherokee at the village. It had been no more difficult to find a business partner already in the land speculation business. Carlson Frye had quite a talent for drafting legal sounding documents and was now on his way to Charleston to insure their business venture would be supported in spite of any objections initiated by Mac's friends in the State Assembly.

Along with establishing business ties, Canfield had also located Bradford's two henchmen who had been in on the original attempt to gain the entire inheritance. Due to the confusing nature of the case against them, they had only recently been sentenced to hang. Canfield had cleverly arranged for their escape from the prison stockade where they were awaiting the hangman's noose. He had sent them off to locate a likely group of settlers. In their search they had come across the group of people from Norfolk who were originally on their way to the Ohio Valley. Stinson had convinced them of the benefits of the Chalequah Valley.

When Canfield finished, she asked, "How'd you know I would come to Iron Mountain?"

"It was a well calculated risk," Canfield smiled confidently. "Little Sparrow assured me that because of Macklin's devotion to his grandparents, any hint of trouble would undoubtedly bring him running. She was fairly certain you would accompany him." Jessica leveled an incredulous gaze at Little Sparrow, who had been standing by silently watching her. "Little Sparrow, how could you possibly be a part of bringing this terrible thing on your own people . . . and Mac?"

"My people are the Cherokee," she replied coldly. "Most of the people at the village are no longer Cherokee. They accept the White ways and White religion. In the battle to come, we Cherokee will rise up and prove ourselves to be the proud people we once were. We will stamp out more of the Whites who would come and take our land."

The Indian woman did not stop there. "If it hadn't been for you, River Walker could have been my own warrior husband. He has it within him to be a great warrior, but you have ruined him."

"Is that why Quiet Bear and Tall Tree were killed? And why you wanted Mac and Oskati dead?" Jess was still unable to comprehend such thinking.

"River Walker was not to have been harmed." Little Sparrow cast an angry glance at Canfield. "He was to have been the only survivor. It is his duty to avenge Quiet Bear's death. Not all of the people will follow Bear Paw, but they will follow River Walker."

"But Quiet Bear was not only your chief, he was your uncle!" Jess countered, her voice choked with emotion.

"He was a weakling, afraid of battle. He would have tried to stop the attack on the settlers. But now," she raised her chin in defiant pride and smiled triumphantly, "now, River Walker will lead the Cherokee into battle."

"What if he doesn't?" Jess glared as her anger overshadowed her fear.

"He will!" Little Sparrow answered with assurance. "It's only fitting that because you took him away from me, you are the reason he'll be mine again."

The young woman pointed to Jess's wrist. "Coyote has taken your bracelet to River Walker. He will tell him that he rode with you to the settlers' camp to try to make them turn back, but the settlers took you captive. He will say he escaped and you gave him your bracelet to take to River Walker. Nothing will stop the attack now.

"The settlers are camped about five miles inside the valley along the river. Tomorrow it will be all over for you, and I will have my warrior back."

"He was never yours to begin with," Jess said coolly, unflinchingly meeting Little Sparrow's piercing gaze.

Just as Little Sparrow raised her hand to strike Jess, Canfield intervened, catching the Indian woman's wrist. "Oh dear," he said sarcastically, "and I thought you wanted to see the world with me. What a disappointment."

Little Sparrow shot a look of contempt at him as she jerked her hand free. Canfield returned a smile of superior complacence.

Remarkably Jess couldn't help but feel a deep pity for the Indian woman. While she resented Little Sparrow's obsessive coveting of her husband, she could understand why any young woman would be attracted to him, and she could imagine the frustration and bitterness facing Little Sparrow's people. The apparently ceaseless tide of White settlers was moving into their hunting grounds, pushing, always pushing. Whether they stood and fought or tried to assimilate the new ways, it was still the same—the White tide incessantly overwhelming them.

"Well now, come along, young lady." Canfield laid his hand on Jessica's shoulder.

"Where are we going?" she asked, pulling away.

"To renew two old acquaintances. Oscar and Johnson will take you back to the settlers' camp. They'll keep you out of sight until the battle tomorrow. "I'll not go into the unpleasant details of what will happen then. It's really too bad it has to be this way," he said, stroking her cheek lightly. "You really are quite lovely."

She turned her head away. Canfield yanked her by the arm and pulled her to her feet.

"What if Mac doesn't fall for your scheme?" she asked defiantly, more angry now than frightened. "He was already upset with me. If he thought I went to the settlers' camp, he might not care to come after me."

"From what I've heard about your Mr. Macklin, he won't stand by and let anyone hold his pretty little wife captive. He'll come . . . and so will the rest of the men in the village."

Pulling back from his grasp, her free hand touched the small oil lamp. Without thinking, she picked up the clay dish and splashed the hot oil on her abductor's left hand. Canfield yelled in pain and released his grip.

Jessica raced for the door. At that moment, a streak of lightning crackled across the night sky and a huge, dark form loomed in front of her, blocking her way. Thunder vibrated through the hills.

"Hold her, Oscar," Canfield grimaced angrily.

"Bet you thought you'd seen the last of me didn't you, little missy!" Jess winced at the voice she remembered from her ordeal at Ellensgate. She looked up at the large man with his wide set jaw and ugly grin. He and his cohort had been agents for British General Clinton during the war. Their mercenary tendencies drew them to working for Bradford Keene more out of a desire for material gain than loyalty to the Crown. Now, inconceivably, she was in their clutches again!

Canfield was wrapping a silk handkerchief around the burn on his hand when he stepped in front of Jessica. Looking down at her with the eye of a hungry cat about to devour a mouse, he surprised her by grinning with something akin to admiration. "Too bad we didn't meet at another time, my dear. I like a lady with spirit. We could have gotten along famously."

"Never in a thousand years," she choked.

Canfield's smile disappeared. "You'd better hurry, Stinson, if you're going to beat the rain. We'll be waiting here for your report tomorrow."

With that, Oscar pulled Jessica outside and led her down the steps.

16

Johnson was mounted and waiting for them. Jess started toward where her own horse was tethered, but Oscar pulled her back saying, "Oh no, ya don't. We're not that stupid. Once up on that horse, you'll be gone and we'll never catch ya. You're riding with me. Up you go."

The big man easily picked her up and set her on his horse sidesaddle fashion. Then he swung up behind her. "There now, isn't that cozy?" he hissed in her ear.

Jess tried to pull away from him, but he held her fast, gripping her wrist tightly with one arm around her waist.

Another flash of lightning lit up the night sky. The horses shied nervously as a thunderclap punctuated the following darkness. The wind was rising. It promised to be a bad storm.

"We should be back here around noon. See ya then, boss," Oscar called back to Canfield who was standing in the doorway.

They started off at a quick trot down the sloping trail. The wind, beginning to whip at the trees, sent brittle dried leaves flying in a driving shower across their dark path.

Another bright flash lighted up the trail for a moment, showing tree branches waving about them in wild, twisting, black silhouettes before the darkness closed in again.

The growing fierceness of the storm heightened the panic rising within Jess. Fighting to keep calm, her mind raced to think of a way to escape. She must be ready if the opportunity presented itself. Mac must be warned of Canfield's scheme before innocent people were hurt. Together they could go to the settlers and somehow they would make them listen and understand they were merely pawns being used in a wild plot to obtain a fortune in jewels by the man they had trusted to bring them to a new Promised Land.

These were certainly ambitious plans for someone held in a lock-tight grip by a thoroughly ruthless man. Her left hand was nearly numb now, and she tried to shield her face from the stinging windblown debris with her right hand.

Again the lightning flashed. The horses whinnied nervously as the thunder seemed to slam into the mountainside with a vengeance. A loud crash sounded as a large tree branch gave way to the tormenting wind.

They were nearly down the trail to the valley floor when Oscar called back to Johnson, "We're almost down to the flat. We'd better ride like the dickens if we're going to beat the rain."

The man's words flew back in his face by the increasing wind. Another crack of thunder made their mounts slow down and begin to skitter nervously sideways. Oscar jerked the reins then spurred his frightened animal forward, but it refused to advance. Another flash of lightning revealed the reason: A large limb had fallen across the trail and blocked their passage.

By this time Johnson had reached them. "Get down and see if you can move it by yourself," Oscar yelled above the gusting wind.

Johnson nodded and dismounted. It was difficult to see him moving about. After a moment, a muffled voice called from the other side of the barrier, "I need a hand here!"

After a few curses, Oscar said, "Come on, missy. You can lend a hand as well." He jumped down from the saddle pulling her with him.

"All right, Johnson, get on the other end there; we'll get this end," he yelled loudly. "Johnson? Johnson!"

No response.

"Where'd that darn fool go now?" he grumbled. "Johnson!"

Jess had been waiting for this moment. In his distraction, Oscar's grip on her wrist slackened. She twisted around sharply to wrench her wrist free and stomp on his foot. Oscar was caught off guard. He grabbed for her, but she darted away out of his reach.

She had taken only four or five steps when a strong arm snatched her off her feet as a powerful hand clamped over her mouth. Jessica was being whisked off to the side of the trail into the deepest shadows of the stormy night! All she could think of was that Johnson was carrying her off into the forest. Frantically she struggled, kicking and trying to bite the strong hand stifling her screams.

"Jess! Jess!" came a whisper in her ear.

So intent in her desperation to free herself, she barely heard the words.

"Jess! Jess! It's me."

It took a minute for the words to sink into her panic-stricken mind. At last they registered, and she stopped struggling. The bear-like hold relaxed, allowing her feet to touch the ground, and the hand came away from her mouth. Jess whirled around to face the tall, solid shadow. "Mac?"

"Jess—" came his wonderful voice through the darkness. "Are you all right?"

"Oh Mac! Yes. Yes!" she cried softly as she threw her arms around his neck.

Mac held his wife close for a long moment, intensely relieved that she was okay. Then, touching a fingertip to her lips, he whispered, "Shhh, stay here."

Jess clung to him tightly. She wanted him to hold her and never let her go, ever again. He had come for her, and no matter what happened now, they were together!

"Jess, it's okay," he whispered in her ear. "Just wait here a minute. I'll be right back."

Reluctantly, she released him. Lightning flashed again just as he turned to go. A scream froze in Jessica's throat when the huge shadow loomed up behind him. In that split second of light, she saw a long, heavy club raised above Mac's head. It was Oscar! The darkness closed over them again. Jess heard the splintering of wood on wood as the club smashed against the tree trunk just behind where Mac had stood a second before.

Mac dived at the club-wielding Oscar and buried his shoulder in the man's mid-section. As they tumbled, Jess could only hear the thudding, bone-jarring blows. Fingers of lightning darted through the night sky to reveal the two shadowed forms wrestling against a tree.

The fierce struggle matched the intensity of the storm and seemed never to end. A brilliant flash of lightning permitted Jess to see Mac swing a smashing blow to Oscar's chin. The big man tottered a moment then crashed to the ground like a falling tree.

154

The last clap of thunder seemed to rend the heavens, and a sudden rush through the leaves brought a deluge of huge icy raindrops. They came in driving sheets that nearly took Jess's breath away.

Jess stumbled toward the place she had last seen Mac standing. Her voice was swallowed up by the noise of the storm. Finally Mac staggered toward her. At last his arms were about her, and they clung to each other in desperate relief. For a few moments they held each other tightly as if reassuring themselves they really were in each other's arms.

Still short of breath, Mac yelled above the roar of the storm. "We've got to get out of this! Come on."

Taking her by the hand, he began leading her away from the trail into the thick of the trees. Mac had been caught out in other storms in this valley, but he couldn't remember any of them being as ferocious as this. He prayed that he would be able to find the one place he knew they could find a safe shelter. It had been years since he had seen the place discovered by his father during a hunting trip before Mac was born. The lightning flashes were coming so close together now, he caught a glimpse of an old familiar landmark and he suddenly knew exactly where they were and how far they had to go. This knowledge and the joy of being reunited with Jess filled him with a renewed energy and he quickened the pace. Jess hurried, trying to keep up, but her skirts kept catching on brambles and branches; the uncertain footing of the forest floor, thick with layers of fallen leaves, caused her to turn her ankle at one point.

The soggy earth seemed to clutch at their feet, making each step an effort as they worked their way up the hillside. Fighting the wind and driving rain, Jessica's strength was nearly spent. Mac put his arm around her to hold her up as they struggled through the trees. At one point she sagged limply, unable to move her exhausted legs another step. Scooping her up in his arms, Mac pressed on until he finally declared breathlessly, "Here we are!"

Peering through the downpour, all she could see when the lightning flashed again was a huge tree over four feet in diameter. Mac carried his wife around the immense girth of the tree trunk. On the opposite side, he ducked down and stepped into a large hole in the trunk. Instantly they were out of the raging storm inside a hollowed-out chamber big enough to stand up in. The dry air inside felt warm and smelled like fresh wood shavings.

"What's this, Mac?" she asked in breathless amazement.

"It's an ancient yellow poplar," he answered, putting her down and holding her until she could stand steady. "Some people call it a tulip tree. This one must be about two or three hundred years old. Here, sit down."

She followed his advice, and he joined her to sit down on the springy, cushion-like floor of the hollowed-out chamber. She scooted closer to him and he closed his arms about her.

"One time when Roger and I were out hunting with our father, we took refuge in here during a sudden storm. No telling how many it has sheltered over the years. Quiet Bear said the Old People believed that the tulip tree volunteered for its heartwood to be hollowed out as a shelter for man. In the beginning the animals became angry with man for killing them, so they decided to bring disease and pestilence against him. The plants overheard the plan and decided to help man by providing medicine to cure the diseases and shelter him in time of need."

"Thank the Lord for the tulip tree," Jess sighed. "Oh Mac, I still can't believe you're here!" She rested her head against his chest and clutched his hand tightly. When he winced, she realized his hand must be bruised from the fight. "Are you okay?"

"I'm fine," he answered, settling back against the wall.

"How'd you know where I was?" she queried, still wondering if she could be dreaming.

"When Coyote gave me your bracelet, I couldn't quite swallow his story." He took another deep breath to catch his wind.

"You knew I wouldn't go to the settlers?" she smiled.

"No. As a matter of fact, Gran said you mentioned such a thing. I could have believed you might try something foolish like that."

"Foolish?" she interrupted, raising her head in mild indignation.

"Foolish," he repeated quietly. She couldn't see his face in the dark, but Jess knew by the rich tone of his voice that he was smiling. Mac gently pressed her head back against his chest. "Foolish, but courageous."

"Then why didn't you believe him?" she asked, thankful for his strong arms holding her close, his warmth chasing the chill away.

"I realized you'd never ask me to bring help after promising Quiet Bear we'd try anything to avoid a fight. It didn't take much persuasion to get Coyote to tell me where you were. I was so angry I scared myself. I guess he thought I might tear him limb from limb if he didn't tell me.

"I was on my way to the cabin when that branch fell in front of me. I'd just gotten down to move it myself when I heard Stinson yell to Johnson."

"What happened to Johnson?" Jess wondered aloud.

"I didn't give him a chance to swing at me," Mac replied. "He'll have a knot on his head when he wakes up."

"I'd begun to think I might never see you again," she choked, trying to swallow the sudden lump in her throat.

He hugged her tighter, reassuring her that everything would be all right.

"Oh Mac, it's all so awful." Jessica was on the verge of tears. "Do you know what's really behind this whole dreadful thing? That horrid jewel collection." Jess explained the scheme as Canfield had related it. Her story simply confirmed what Mac had guessed. Mac told Jess about his talk with Hampton and Smythe.

"What are we to do?" she asked softly, her weariness overtaking her.

"Rest now." His voice was soothing. "This storm has set in for the time being. It won't be dawn for a couple of hours, and no one will be able to do anything for a while this morning."

"Mac—"

"Hmmm?"

"Please forgive me for doubting you would do the right thing. Gran said you'd never lead an attack on the settlers. I should have known you wouldn't. It was just that you were so enraged and I really couldn't blame you, but I . . . I was afraid you were angry enough to do such a thing."

He was silent a long moment. "I hate to admit it now, but if it hadn't been for your persistence in making me stop and think before I talked with the rest of the men in the village, I might have. After seeing that look in your eyes, I knew if I went ahead with the attack, things would never be the same between us. You do understand, though, I will stand with the men in defense of the village."

"Yes, I know, and I'll stand with you," she vowed sleepily as she snuggled closer.

Jess was exhausted, and although the storm still raged outside and the trouble between the White settlers and the Cherokee village was still imminent, she felt secure in Mac's arms once more. The storm between them was over. They would be working together again. Being cold, soaked to the skin, tired, and hungry couldn't dampen the joy brought by that realization.

Mac was so relieved to have her safely beside him again that he said a prayer of thanksgiving. He realized the mistake he had made. In his effort to protect her, he had tried to shut her out. It was an adjustment he was going to have to make after being so much of a loner for such a long time. Now, Mac realized that his wife had taken very seriously her vow to stand by him through thick and thin. They were one, and that meant they would share the troubles as well as the triumphs. Somehow that knowledge gave him a more optimistic outlook than he'd had for a long time. He still meant to protect her from trouble, but he intended to communicate a little better from now on.

17

Jess was awakened by a furious chattering noise. She blinked a couple of times to clear her vision and saw a small red squirrel poised just outside the hollow, scolding the human intruders. Because of its variety of chattering noises, the creature had earned the nickname "mountain boomer," and they had apparently invaded its storehouse.

The memory of the stormy night came back clearly. Jess didn't want to move for fear of waking Mac, whose arm was still curled over her.

She could see the interior of their living shelter and was surprised by the size of it. She looked up to a height of about eight feet. The ceiling was illuminated by the early morning sunlight and looked like thick panels of irregular curtains where the forces of deterioration had eaten deep grooves into the heartwood.

Mac stirred, awakened by the insistent little squirrel. His wife was immediately appalled by the sight of his face. One eye was cut and surrounded with a dark bruise that nearly caused it to be swollen shut. The right side of his lower lip was also cut and swollen.

"Oh Mac, your poor face!" she gasped, touching his chin gingerly.

"I know it's not that great, but it never seemed to bother you that much before," he responded sleepily.

"Mac—" she smiled with slight exasperation at his teasing, "you look awful. Does it hurt badly?"

"Only if I move," he groaned with a lopsided grin. "That fella has quite a punch. How're you?"

"Fine. I was just thinking about breakfast. Looks like we spoiled that little fellow's plans for his morning meal." The squirrel had scampered away a few feet but continued his persistent scolding.

"I think you're right. Well, Mrs. Macklin, as much as I enjoy being cuddled up with you in this cozy little nest, I'm afraid we have some traveling we must do."

"What do you have in mind?" she asked, getting to her feet stiffly.

Mac groaned slightly and held his side as he got to his feet. "Let's get outside first."

"Are you sure you're all right?" she asked as they ducked down and out through the opening.

"Just a couple of bruised ribs," he answered, straightening up and looking around. "That was some storm last night."

They breathed deeply of the sparkling, cool air. It was fragrantly fresh. Here and there droplets of rainwater glistened like jewels highlighted by the slanted rays of dawn filtering through the foliage. The forest floor was littered with broken tree limbs and piles of leaves collected in little drifts of debris around roots and bushes.

Jess noticed her damp skirt was tattered along its hem, and her lovely pink silk blouse was mud-splattered with the right sleeve torn from shoulder to elbow. "I must be a sight," she said, brushing her hair back from her dirt-smudged face.

At that moment, Mac's heart was filled with love and thankfulness. He touched her face softly. With a nod and a wink he said quietly, "Aye, that ye are, lass." The look in his eyes was the same look she had seen when they exchanged their wedding vows, and it quickened her pulse. Even the clear trilling of a mockingbird perched in a nearby tree couldn't match the singing in her heart.

Suddenly Mac remembered something. "By the way, would you like this back?" He pulled her bracelet out of his hunting shirt pocket and slipped it on her outstretched wrist. She reached up to place a gentle kiss on the uninjured side of his mouth. Enclosing her in his arms, Mac held his wife tightly for a long moment. They were thankful to be together.

"We'd better get started," he finally said. "My horse is probably back at the village by this time. I'll wager Stinson and Johnson went on back to the cabin when they came around. Did Canfield and Little Sparrow come on horseback or by buggy?"

"Buggy. Canfield mentioned it just after they got there. And the horse I rode was still there," she answered.

Mac looked around thoughtfully. "We're not far from the cabin, so we'll have to take a chance on getting the horse. We could never make it to the settlers' camp in time on foot. Do you think you can make it to the cabin with your sore ankle?"

She nodded, "It seems better this morning."

The sun had just barely climbed above the eastern rim of the valley as they began trudging along the sodden forest floor. For nearly half an hour they worked their way through the trees. After struggling through a narrow tan-

162

gle of rhododendron bushes barring the way, they stopped to catch their breath.

As they rested, the delicious aroma of coffee and bacon wafted by them on the rain-washed air. Jess was so hungry she would almost have chewed on a piece of pine bark. The smell of breakfast was torturous and she felt lightheaded. Closing her eyes a moment as they sat side by side on a fallen tree trunk, she tried to clear her senses and dismiss the thought of food.

"Jess—" Mac's voice was low and warning as he touched her hand, "don't move."

A large black bear lumbered out of the brush across the small clearing in front of them. Its small shiny black eyes had not noticed them. His head was held high, turning this way and that, sniffing at the aromatic breeze. The animal was looking for breakfast too, and cooked or raw made little difference to him.

Bristly black fur bulged over a body obviously storing abundant fat for the hibernation coming soon. Taking two more steps into the clearing, the bear's first sight of Jessica and Mac startled him. With remarkable agility for a creature his size, he sidestepped and stopped to stare at them, still unsure of what he was seeing.

Mac and Jess held their breath. Jess tried not to pay any attention to the long, black claws that looked like curved steel. She and Robbie had once witnessed a she-bear, desperate for food to feed her twin cubs, attack a large doe caught in a tangle of bramble vines. One lethal swipe of those terrible claws had provided dinner for the cubs that day.

Mac and Jess both knew bears could be very unpredictable, and this one was taking a long time to look them over. The animal made three warning woofing sounds and

163

lunged forward, then stopped. Jess cringed but remained still.

Very slowly Mac edged in front of her and whispered, "When I'm blocking his view, reach for the knife in my boot and put it in my hand."

Jess bent down very slightly, trying not to make much movement, and grasped the knife's handle. As she placed it in Mac's hand, the bear rushed forward again, this time charging directly at them. Then suddenly he made a right-angle turn and lumbered off through the brush. The bushes closed about him, and he was gone like a dark vapor.

Mac let out a long sigh of relief as Jess tried to catch her breath. They had heard of such bear behavior before. The charge was a warning and not a true attack. Having given notice of his ferocity, he had decided that although they had startled him, the human intruders were not a real threat and he need not waste his energy any further.

"Thank you, Lord," Jess breathed. Mac nodded an "Amen." Without another word, the two of them began moving toward the cabin once more, still weak in the knees from the experience.

With his fingers to his lips Mac signaled Jess to be very quiet. When they could finally see the roof and smoke curling out of the chimney, Mac led her through the last few trees. Stopping at the edge of the clearing on the south side of the cabin, he motioned for her to wait while he crept silently up to the porch. After their encounter with the bear, she wasn't sure she wanted to wait there by herself, but she said nothing and watched Mac move away as silently as a shadow. Once on the porch, he ducked under an open window and peeked in to see who was inside.

Little Sparrow, Canfield, and Stinson sat at the table. A disgruntled Johnson dished up their breakfast.

At last Mac signaled to her to join him on the porch. Ever so quietly, he pointed toward the wooden bar that locked the shutter. She understood his message: Wait until he had barred the door then do the same with the shutters.

Without a sound, Mac slipped the heavy door latch into place, locking it from the outside. Moving to the other window, Mac signaled to Jess. They quickly pulled the shutters closed and fastened them. Instantly there was scrambling inside as the occupants suddenly realized the tables had been turned. Their four prisoners pounded on the door shouting curses.

Mac grinned at Jess and patted her shoulder. "That was almost too easy." The thought was slightly disquieting, but he shook it off. "We'll come back for them later and take them over to the constable at Ellensgate."

The two of them scurried over to the light buggy. They could see that Canfield had not unhitched the poor horse. Standing in a three-legged pose with one hind foot barely touching the ground, the animal looked bedraggled after having stood in his traces through the night.

Mac gave Jess a hand up. As he turned the buggy toward the trail, she quipped, "Too bad we don't have time for breakfast."

"If Tobias Alder doesn't shoot us first, maybe he'll share a cup of coffee with us." With that, Mac whistled to the horse and they rode quickly down the trail.

Jess glanced back at the cabin. The four angry captives would have to sit and consider their misdeeds—a large black bear ambled somewhere nearby looking for a few more meals before his long winter's nap.

Neither Mac nor Jessica minded leaving the Sycamore Creek cabin at all this time.

18

Although the muddy trail made slippery footing for the horse, they made fairly good time and reached the settlers' campsite within the hour.

The camp had suffered badly from the storm. Two wagons had been stripped of their canvas covering. The shattered hulk of one wagon lay smashed against a huge boulder at the edge of the river. Remnants of another could be seen strewn farther downstream.

At the moment, the entire group of settlers was gathered on the bank of the river, their attention focused at something on the other side.

Mac pulled the buggy up to the crowd and stopped. "What's going on?"

A man standing nearby pointed across the river. "Over yonder, the McCullough boy's caught up in the tree. The river came up all of a sudden in the storm and washed three of the wagons off. Lost two men sleepin' under one of them. Ever'body got out of the McCullough wagon except the boy there. Got himself up in that tree and that's what saved him. But now we can't get to him."

Mac hopped to the ground and helped Jess down. They made their way through the crowd. At the river's edge they stood next to the man Mac had met before. Tobias Alder turned.

"What are you doing here?" he asked suspiciously. "Can't you see we've trouble enough right now?"

"Do you have a long rope?" Mac asked, ignoring the question.

"We tried throwing one to him, but he nearly fell trying to catch it. Even if he could catch it, how could it help? He's only six and probably couldn't tie it off if he tried. We even tried a human chain, but the current nearly swept two more men away."

"Where's the rope?" Mac asked. "Do you have a hatchet handy?"

Alder studied Mac for a moment then picked up the rope and called for a hatchet. Someone handed him the hatchet, and Mac quickly tied the rope in a solid knot around the hatchet handle.

"What's the boy's name?" Mac asked as he worked.

"Thaddeus," Alder said, watching him curiously. "That's his pa there. Broke his arm when the wagon went over, but he got his other youngster and wife out."

Mac glanced at the father only a little older than himself standing at the river's edge and clutching his arm in a sling, watching his son helplessly. His young wife clung to him fearfully, not wanting to look yet unable to turn away from the terrifying sight of her little boy in such a precarious situation.

During the storm the river had gone on a rampage, rising nearly fifteen feet in a matter of minutes as rain from the hills gathered in a wild runoff. Although it had retreated to its banks, it still ran muddy and swift. At this point it was about ten yards wide and four to ten feet deep.

"Thaddeus!" Mac yelled across the noisily rushing torrent. "I'm going to throw this rope over, but don't try to catch it! Let it lodge in the branch beside you before you take hold of it!"

"What if you hit the boy?" Alder asked nervously.

"Would you like to do it?" Mac held out the hatchet to him.

The older man stepped back. "No."

Mac handed the other end of the rope to Alder and prepared for the throw. The hatchet was clumsy, not balanced like a tomahawk, and the rope made it heavier still.

Taking careful aim, he noticed Jess's head bowed. He said a quick prayer as well. Then taking as deep a breath possible with his sore ribs, he summoned all his strength and let the hatchet fly. At first the crowd of onlookers gasped, then everyone cheered as the blade sunk solidly into a large branch just a foot to the right of the boy.

"Thaddeus!" Mac called again. "When you reach for the hatchet, grab the rope first and hold it tight! Then pull the hatchet out!"

Everyone waited nervously as the little child scooted down the branch and took hold of the rope. He retrieved the hatchet.

"Wrap it 'round the branch next to you! That's it! Now make a loop in the rope and put the hatchet through it . . . a little bigger loop . . . bigger . . . That's it! Now, drop the hatchet down through the loop! Good . . . good boy! Okay, now just hang on a little longer!"

Mac turned to Alder. "We need to tie off that end good and tight."

168

One of the others helped Alder secure the end of the rope around a sturdy young oak growing along the bank.

Mac turned toward Jess. She walked over and kissed his cheek. "I wish they'd named you Safely Standing at Home instead of River Walker."

When he grinned rather ruefully, she quickly added, "But if it can be done, you'd be the one I'd trust to do it. After all, what's one little river crossing and rescue after everything else that's happened these past two days!"

Mac nodded and took hold of the rope, pulling on it with all his weight to be certain both ends were secure. He moved out into the swirling stream. Slowly inching his way toward the middle, he pulled himself hand-over-hand along the rope when the water was too swift and deep to stand.

The swirling current tugged at him relentlessly. The muddy water splashed in his face, stinging the cuts and blurring his vision. At one point, some floating debris narrowly missed slamming into him. As he approached the other side, he worked his way up the rope that angled up toward the tree. Finally he had inched high enough to escape the rushing water. Focusing on the child's face, he tried to ignore the pain in his rib cage and his hands.

When he finally reached the tree, Mac realized that the rope was tied out on the limb too far for him to gain his footing. Instead he would have to swing up on the limb where Thaddeus was now clinging with one hand and reaching hopefully toward his rescuer. Just as Mac reached for the limb, the rope suddenly sagged without warning and Mac dropped lower, swinging precariously by one hand. The crowd gasped as he tried to swing around enough to grab the rope with both hands. At last he was able to grip the lifeline with his free hand, but his feet were again only inches above the swift stream and the pain in his ribs made him gasp for breath.

"The tree!" someone shouted, and everyone turned to see the oak tree where the other end of the rope had been anchored tilting at an angle toward the rushing water. The debris at the base of the tree had hidden the fact the flood waters had washed away the riverbank, undermining the roots.

"Quick, men, grab the rope!" Alder commanded.

The sound of rending wood echoed above the rushing water as thick roots were being twisted and slipped from their weakened anchorage along the bank. It took a moment for the men to react. At last they rushed to where the tree was leaning even more drastically now.

Mac sank closer to the turbulent water below. With each swinging movement, he tried to get back to the tree and Thaddeus, but the anchor tree loosened its grip from the bank.

The men realized they would never be able to hold the tree to prevent it from falling into the river. The tremendous strain would most likely snap the limb where the boy waited and send both of them plummeting into the rampaging waters.

"Dear Lord, help them," Jess choked frantically as she watched the group trying to steady the tree. Looking back toward Mac, she could hear him shouting, "Cut the rope!" The men were too busy to hear, so she ran toward Alder screaming, "He wants you to cut the rope from this tree! Hurry!"

Alder looked to Mac. "Cut the rope!" he shouted again.

One of the men pulled a large hunting knife from a sheath on his belt and began sawing at the rope near the knot. When it snapped free, Mac swung the short distance to the trunk of the tree and grabbed a stout branch. He pulled himself up onto the branch and leaned back against the trunk to rest a moment.

Jess's knees were shaking so badly she sank down on a nearby wooden crate. Out of the corner of her eye, she caught movement. She turned just in time to see the oak tree splash into the stream. It hesitated a moment, then was swept downstream by the overwhelming power of the current as if it were a mere broken branch. Jess watched awestruck by the sheer power of the ceaseless stream. From that day on, she would always be wary of a deep swift river, never able to forget completely how close it had come to taking Mac from her.

She breathed a prayer of thanksgiving. For the moment she was satisfied. Mac was on dry land, and he would probably help the child down, then walk back to the place where the settlers had forded and wait for a wagon to come across for them.

On the other side, Mac climbed up to where young Thaddeus clung patiently waiting for his rescue. Pulling himself up, the man settled on the limb next to the boy. The boy smiled and nodded his head at what Mac was saying to him, and he grasped Mac's hand for reassurance.

After a minute, Mac reached over and untied the rope and hatchet from the limb and swung them so they dropped to the ground about two yards from the base of the tree, away from the river's edge. Thaddeus climbed onto his back and hugged his neck tightly; then they began their descent.

A collective sigh of relief escaped the crowd as it watched them reach the ground safely. Mac knelt down, and Thaddeus hesitated a moment as if he wanted to be certain they were safe.

Jessica looked at Tobias Alder who had come to stand beside her. "Do you think the buggy could make it across the ford to pick them up?" she asked.

He looked at her blankly then shook his head. "This is the ford, ma'am. There's no way to get a buggy or horse across with the river like it is now. They'll either have to camp there 'til the river goes back down or make their way downstream for a place to cross."

"But that would take hours." She felt a growing concern as she considered the possibility of Bear Paw's renegades mounting an attack at any time.

"At least," Alder began to agree, then looked over at Mac. "What's he up to now?"

Mac was busily chopping a large limb from the tree they had just climbed down. For the better part of the next hour, he worked. When he had finally completed his task, he had cut two lengths of the limb, each about four feet in length, and lashed them together with wood vines cut from the branches of another tree. He had cut away all of the foliage from it except a short section at the end of one timber where the limb had branched in two and formed a fork. At the base of this fork, Mac tied one end of the rope, which he had pulled over to their side, then he retied the hatchet to the other end.

Everyone, including those who were busy trying to put their wagons back in order, stopped and watched curiously as the young man took off his jacket and placed it on the boy. With the sleeves dragging the ground, it nearly swallowed little Thaddeus. Mac knelt down and the youngster climbed on his back. Mac pulled the jacket sleeves around in front and tied the loose ends across his chest, securing the child in papoose fashion so he would not be swept from his back. Mac fully intended to recross the river right there.

Jess couldn't believe it. What could he be thinking? How would he ever be able to fight against the current and float across on his makeshift raft?

Mac picked up his hatchet again and called to the settlers, "Line coming across!"

He began swinging the hatchet in a circle over his head, increasing the size of the circle until the right moment. He then let it fly. The settlers scattered as the hatchet came sailing across, carrying the end of the rope with it. As soon as it landed, one of the men snatched it up.

Five, then six men took hold of the rope. As Mac signaled from the other side, they slowly pulled up the slack until they were dragging the narrow raft toward the river's edge. When it reached the water, Mac stepped into the shallow eddy, grasping the two prongs of the forked end of the limb as a cattle drover might grab the horns of a steer. Then, stepping deeper into the swirling current he quickly swung his other leg over the crude raft and held on tightly with Thaddeus securely in place on his back.

Immediately the current began sweeping them downstream, but the settlers had begun pulling the moment Mac and the boy had settled on the makeshift raft. Within less than a minute, the two of them were swept in a wide arc across the river, coming to rest at the river's edge only fifteen yards downstream from where the people were waiting.

Everyone rushed forward. The camp came alive with whoops and hollers and cheers. The mother and father clutched their child between them. Jessica ran to Mac and threw her arms around his neck, hugging him tightly as the rest of the crowd slapped him on the back with congratulations and thanks.

The McCulloughs were so choked with emotion they could barely speak, but Mac understood and patted the youngster on the head. "He's a brave lad, and he ties a good knot, too."

The boy, still clinging to his father, returned a smile.

Alder pushed through the crowd. "My wife has some coffee. Come over here by the fire."

Jessica and Mac followed him and sat down on the large trunk he offered as a chair.

"Macklin, that was the most amazing thing I've ever seen. We thought you were a goner there for a minute when that tree went down. I . . . I'm afraid I may have been thinking some mighty unfair things about you. I, uh . . . want to apologize. How'd you ever think of a raft like that?"

As Mac accepted the blanket Mrs. Alder handed to him and wrapped it around his shoulders, he replied, "There wasn't time to go downstream. After you've been out here a while, you'll learn to make do with whatever's at hand."

"That sounds encouraging," Alder smiled cautiously. "Does that mean your people are moving off our land?"

Alder's comment reminded them of the impending conflict. In all of the excitement, Mac and Jess had nearly forgotten their purpose in coming. The young couple exchanged glances as they sipped the coffee Mrs. Alder had given to them. Mac shook his head slowly. "Alder, my wife and I have a rather complicated story to tell you."

Alder and his wife listened silently as they related the entire story. The Alders clasped hands as the realization of their situation settled heavily upon them. After Mac had finished, they silently stared at the campfire crackling before them.

Alder finally stood up and began kicking angrily at an imaginary target. "Tarnation, if I get my hands on Frye and Canfield, I'll wring their blasted necks."

The man looked at his storm-ravaged camp where people were still gathering rain-soaked items blown by the wind. "Look at 'em, Macklin. They're at the end of their rope. They're decent, hardworking people. What am I going to tell them now? We don't have money or provisions to go anywhere else, and winter'll soon be on us. This was our chance for a new start—a chance to build our own town—clean, with room to grow, with a school and a church. What am I going to tell them now?"

As he spoke, Mac had a thought. "Mr. Alder, there's the north end of the valley. With a little work, it can be as productive as the settlement land."

The settlers' leader looked him squarely in the eye. "You mean settle in *here*, with the Cherokee? In the same valley?" He shook his head. "I don't know about that. I mean, how could we be sure they wouldn't rise up and scalp us all in our beds?"

"That's probably the first question they'll ask about you folks when we mention the idea to them!" Mac mused. "Especially after the murder of Quiet Bear and Tall Tree."

The gray-haired man sighed deeply, "I see what you mean. Will they believe we had nothing to do with that?" he asked, rubbing his chin thoughtfully.

"If you turn over the men who did it, that might help," Mac replied with a hint of irritation. The memory of the ambush had rekindled his anger, but he was at last in control of it.

"Well, I can't say for sure, but aside from Johnson and Stinson only two others rode out after your party left the other day: Mo Tilson and Dick Keller."

"Where are they?" Mac wanted to know.

"Seems they've already reaped what they sowed. We pulled their bodies from the river this morning. They were bedded down under one of the wagons that got washed away."

Jessica spoke up. "Mr. Alder, why don't you come to the village and speak with the Council. Most of them only want to live in peace in their own village," she suggested.

"Most of them?" Alder asked, still having difficulty accepting the idea.

"A promise was made to Quiet Bear just before he died," Mac said, taking Jess's hand, pride and deep affection shining in his dark eyes. "The Council will respect that promise for a peaceful solution if they can be sure you will do the same."

Jess didn't hear Alder's response. She seemed lost in the dark depths of Mac's eyes when suddenly the whole world turned crazily upside down. The next thing she knew, she was lying in the back of one of the wagons. A soothing voice reminded her of her mother. "There now, dear. You'll be fine in a minute." She looked up to see Mrs. Alder standing beside her.

"My goodness," Jess said, still a little dazed. "What happened?"

"You fainted, but you'll be fine." The older woman patted her arm. "You scared your poor husband though. He's right outside. Mr. Macklin, she's okay now."

Mac climbed quickly into the wagon and knelt beside her, taking her hand. "Jess, are you all right?" He looked pale and quite distressed.

"I'm fine. Guess we should have stopped and had breakfast with Little Sparrow after all," she smiled, trying to reassure him.

"This must be your first," Mrs. Alder smiled.

"First?" Jess asked in bewilderment.

"First baby," Mrs. Alder laughed gently.

"Baby?" Jess and Mac chorused.

"Mr. Macklin said you'd been very tired lately and not feeling well, especially in the mornings. You look perfectly healthy otherwise and unless you're in the habit of fainting at the drop of a hat, I'd say you are going to have a new addition to your family.

"I ought to recognize the symptoms by now. Two of those families out there are two of our eight children with six of our twenty-three grandchildren! Congratulations to you both." With that the woman smiled and made a discreet exit leaving the young couple alone to let the idea sink in.

19

Shortly after noon, they rode slowly along the trail toward the village. Jessica rested her head on Mac's shoulder. Tobias Alder and two of the other men from the camp rode behind the buggy.

"I can hardly believe it—a baby," Jess smiled contentedly. "I think I've suspected it for a little while, but with all the trouble, I was almost afraid to mention it."

"You might have let me in on it."

Mac sounded a bit perturbed, and she looked up at him curiously. He looked down at her rather sternly, but when she began to muster her defense, a big grin slowly lit up his face and his dark eyes crinkled with merriment. Although the grin caused pain from his split lip, it was nearly impossible to suppress the smile.

"Mac!" She scolded his teasing then happily laid her head against his shoulder again. She would never forget the moment in the Alders' wagon when they had both discovered the wonderful news. In all of their time together, through the pain and sadness they had experienced, even with Quiet Bear's death, he had never shed a tear. But as they had stared at each other in wonder, with the realization that she was carrying his child, Mac had blinked back tears of joy.

"Uh-oh," he said, bringing her back to the present.

"What's the matter?" she asked with sudden apprehension.

"You remember Sergeant Arnham?"

Sergeant Arnham was an old army friend of Jessica's father, who had served with him in India. Mac and Jess had encountered him leading a British patrol on their trip to Charleston just after they'd first met. Months later when Mac was taken prisoner by the British, Sergeant Arnham had helped him escape. "Sergeant Arnham? Yes, of course I remember him. Why do you ask about him?"

"When I escaped from Fort Winnsboro, I sort of made a promise that we'd name our first son after him." He looked straight ahead as he spoke, daring to look at her only after she remained silent.

"So that's why you asked me what his first name was that day at Sir Gaston's!" she exclaimed. "Aloysius? Oh Mac—what about as a middle name? How does Roger Aloysius Macklin sound?"

He looked at her in questioning silence, and from the expression of deep pleasure that appeared in his dark eyes, she knew he was touched by her suggestion to name their son after Mac's late brother.

A twinkle came to his eye and he said, "We can always call him Ram for short. If he inherits his mother's stubbornness, it ought to be a fitting name."

"There you go again, calling me stubborn," she protested lightly, too happy to really take offense. "I'm *not* stubborn!"

"You're without a doubt the most wonderful girl in the world, Jess, but you *are* stubborn," he grinned.

"I'm not," she insisted indignantly.

"Okay, who was it that was so determined to make the trip to Charleston that she was ready to hire a twelve-year-old boy to help her drive the wagons?"

"I really had no choice."

"Who was it that risked life and limb to save a family keepsake from being destroyed by fire?"

"Maybe that was a little foolish, but it was the shawl Gran had given me, and it had been from her wedding. I couldn't—"

His voice lowered a bit as he looked down at her, his steady gaze meeting hers. "And who was it that persisted so, she finally got through her husband's mindless fury and prevented him from making a terrible mistake?"

She looked up into his handsome face, carrying the battle scars of his fight to rescue her. For someone who was so expert at masking his feelings, the expression of adoration and gratitude in his eyes was unmistakable, and no further words between them were required. Jess was speechless with joy. Their relationship had been restored and even strengthened by the ordeal they had just experienced.

Finally breaking the silence, Jess asked saucily, "By the way, darling, what makes you so sure the baby will be a boy anyway?"

He chuckled and put his arm around her. "Well, if it's a girl, we won't have to call her Aloysius, will we!"

She loved laughing with him.

The villagers were relieved to see Mac had brought Jessica back safe and sound, but they eyed Tobias Alder and his companions suspiciously. They told Mac that the village hadn't suffered from the storm's fury and that Oskati had taken several of the men to check on the well-being of the families at the High Meadow camp.

Mac took Jessica by his grandparents' home then led Alder's party down to the meetinghouse. He planned to speak with the three remaining Council members and the rest of the men who had stayed at the village.

Mac presented the story of the plot to send the Cherokee on the warpath. The Council chose six men to ride to Sycamore Creek cabin to bring back the four people there. One of the young men who had originally been on Bear Paw's side alerted the Council to the fact that Bear Paw, Mitakiah, Coyote, and three others had left the village shortly after Jess and Mac returned. With this information, the Council advised the posse to make haste in case the troublemakers were going to try to help Little Sparrow and the others get away.

After a lengthy discussion, the Council members finally agreed to allow the settlers to occupy the land at the northern end of the valley during the winter months, if they promised not to extend their boundaries southward beyond the halfway point. The winter would prove a trial period for them. When spring came, if there had been problems between them, the settlers would be ushered on their way. Alder and his men left slightly apprehensive about the tenuous peace that had been established but relieved that for the present things were working out without bloodshed.

If not for the lingering sadness over the loss of Quiet Bear, the mood around the dinner table that night would have been quite festive. Grandfather was feeling much better. He and Gran were elated over the news about the

181

baby and much relieved with the way everything seemed to be working out with the settlers.

Melden was still quite sullen over the fact that Mac had refused to allow him to ride along to Sycamore Creek cabin to find Jessica. He'd been insulted when Mac told him in no uncertain terms that his presence would be more hindrance than help. While Hampton had taken the opportunity to learn about the Cherokee culture from Grandfather Macklin, Melden spent the time waiting for Mac's return by either pacing nervously back and forth or sitting on the porch with his feet propped up, watching the trail wind up from the valley floor.

Now young Hampton seemed to be enjoying himself fully. Their mission had been accomplished with Jessica's signature safely on the documents he carried and he was enjoying one of the best wild plum puddings he had ever tasted in his life.

Later they enjoyed a cup of after-dinner coffee as they listened to young Hampton's detailed account of his travels in the New World. With a wry sense of humor, he related the various trials he and Melden had been through. Soon he had everyone laughing as he described, a bit to Melden's chagrin, the destructive brawl in the village tavern.

"And then this rather stout—extremely stout—barmaid crept up behind him and smashed him on the back of the head with an iron skillet! I was certain we'd both be boiled in oil. As it was, the sheriff carted Melden off to jail, and I languished in that exceedingly wretched inn for three days. Of course if I hadn't become ill with the ague, I would never have had to stop later on to recover and would never have met Lucianna." The storyteller fell silent, musing pleasantly over his memories of the doctor's lovely young daughter. The events now appeared to be more of an adventure, and little by little, the young man was beginning to appreciate this new way of life. Just a month earlier, he would have scoffed at the slightest suggestion that such a change would take place.

A rapid knock at the door interrupted the young man's stories. Mac went to answer it. Oskati's cousin stood on the porch and solemnly announced, "The men are back from Sycamore Creek. You'd better come."

The gravity in his voice immediately set everyone on alert.

"What's wrong, Had-atá?"

The young man looked past him to the group inside and repeated, "You just better come quickly."

Jess and Melden joined Mac at the door. Mac turned and said, "Jess, wait here." Melden didn't wait for an invitation. He immediately followed Mac out the door.

Jessica followed them out onto the porch and watched their shadowed forms fade off into the darkness down the path to the village.

Hampton stepped outside to stand beside her. "Really, Mrs. Macklin, is life always like this here in the colonies . . . One crisis falling upon another?"

"Goodness no, Mr. Hampton. Sometimes we go more than a day without a major crisis."

He looked at her a moment then she smiled. "Ahhh yes, of course, you're speaking facetiously." Becoming serious, he continued, "I don't mean to be impertinent, Mrs. Macklin, but how does a young woman of obvious refinement as yourself manage to endure the life here? I mean with your inheritance from Sir Gaston, you're a very wealthy young woman even after giving away the jewel collection. You could live anywhere in the world. Why do you stay in this primitive country?"

Jess studied him for a moment, sensing that he was curious in a sensitive way, not with the haughtiness one might expect.

The eastern hills were black against a deep, slate gray sky that grew a shade lighter as the large disk of the harvest moon began to rise. "Well, Mr. Hampton," she began thoughtfully as she looked out over the valley lying quiet in the darkness, "I suppose I might appear to be a rather odd duck when you put it that way. But this country is my home. Even with all its dangers and hardships, I love it. I can't imagine being cooped up in some crowded city, no matter how grand.

"I realize money can be very helpful, but I've seen what can happen when people become obsessed with their wealth. I don't want that to happen to us. Andrew Macklin has made my life richer than any fortune ever could. Twice now our lives have been jeopardized because of that money. As far as I'm concerned, it's really been more of a burden than a blessing."

"Well, Mrs. Macklin, I'll be happy to relieve you of that burden."

Jess whirled around at the sound of the chilling voice behind her.

20

"Mr. Frye!" she gasped.

"Canfield?" Hampton exclaimed in surprise as he noticed the pistol in the man's hand.

"Not Canfield," Jessica corrected. "This is Carlson Frye. What are you doing here? Canfield said you were on the way to Charleston."

In the glow of light from the window, his face was set in hard lean lines that indicated he meant business. The man ignored her question and whispered harshly, "Quiet! Both of you. Move along there to the side of the house."

Gone was the smooth-talking, polite facade presented by Frye at their earlier meeting. His cold impatience signaled to Jess that he was in an extremely dangerous mood.

The two slowly obeyed his order. The man glanced around to make certain they weren't being observed. Gran and Grandfather were still sitting by the fire; they had remained inside when Jess and Hampton had gone out and were now completely unaware of the third person's presence.

As they moved into the shadows along the side of the house, Hampton whispered nervously, "I hate to contradict you, Mrs. Macklin, but this is Howard Canfield. Anyone in Cheltenham can verify that."

"What? I don't understand. Canfield said he was—"

"My astute business partner posing as Howard Canfield. I can understand your confusion," the man Jess knew as Frye said with slight amusement. "Actually, he was an actor by the name of Emory Crane. I hired him in London. Originally, he was to pose as me until you were taken care of. It was to appear that an impostor had put you out of the way, intent upon gaining the jewel collection for himself. I'm afraid he began taking his role too seriously and intended to write me out of the script. Of course, it could be he realized he was in for a fatal accident that would erase any tangible connection with me. I assumed the identity of Carlson Frye to keep a close hand on the situation without implicating my true self in any way."

"But the land company—" Jessica was still finding it difficult to accept this new twist. "Mac said the Fair View Land Company was well known to the State Assembly, and you, or at least Carlson Frye, had several friends there."

"I dare say the poor fellow we found alongside the trail did, but his friends wouldn't have recognized him. We couldn't be sure if he'd been the victim of an Indian attack or some wild animal. However, his letters and identification were intact and provided the perfect setup for us. It couldn't have happened more perfectly if I had planned it myself.

"When it was all over, Frye was simply to have faded off into the far country and I, Howard Canfield, was to return from a trip on the Continent to find that Sir Gaston's heiress had perished before signing the collection over to the museum.

"Harold Smythe would have testified that a man claiming to be Howard Canfield had contacted him in the attempt to locate you, Jessica. To the Macklins and Little Sparrow, he was calling himself Howard Canfield and planning the uprising to dispose of you and claim the jewels for himself. I would have appeared quite shocked that someone would actually assume my identity for such a grisly purpose. Of course, I would have appeared appropriately distraught with your cruel fate. However, everyone at home knows I'm not especially fond of museums and wouldn't have been surprised when I decided to keep the collection myself. Just keep moving there."

"Where are we going?" Hampton asked miserably.

"We're taking this back trail over the mountain to what is left of Uncle Gaston's estate. I've been using it as my headquarters. The local people think it's haunted and stay far away, allowing me to come and go as I please. I had a restful night's sleep last night after I got the message that you'd been caught in our little snare, Mrs. Macklin. I slipped back over here tonight to check on the success my actor friend and the Indian woman achieved. You can imagine my disappointment to learn they bungled things so badly."

Jessica stopped stock-still in her tracks, causing Canfield nearly to crash into her.

"Get going," he ordered impatiently.

"No!" Taking a deep breath, she stiffened her back.

"What? I said get going." He pressed the pistol against her side.

She winced with the pressure of the steel barrel but took a deep breath. "If you're going to kill me anyway, you may as well do it here. I'm not going a step farther. Besides, I've already signed the jewels over to the museum."

They had walked about twenty yards from the cabin and were standing underneath the spreading branches of a tall pine tree. The moon had climbed high enough to send its cool light streaming over the valley. It cast an eerie bristling shadow of pine needles across the trio. In the pale light, Hampton watched Jessica with nervous admiration for taking a daring stand, but he feared Canfield's reaction.

"Canfield, really," Hampton finally spoke up, his voice a bit shaky. "How do you possibly expect to get away with this? She has already signed them over, so you may as well just let us go and be on your way."

"I know she has," Canfield replied irritably. "I've been watching through the window for quite some time trying to decide what to do. I'll admit, Hampton, you were an unexpected obstacle, but you'll come in handy to carry my ransom demand to Smythe. Smythe will simply have to draw up new papers turning the jewels over to me. Jessica will accompany me to Charleston to assure my safe arrival. I shall sail to Amsterdam, travel to Vienna, collect the jewels before anyone over there is the wiser, and find some wonderful secluded castle, perhaps along the Rhine, and live out my days in luxury."

"You're mad," Hampton declared.

"Perhaps, but I shall enjoy my madness in wealthy ease," Canfield mused. "Actually, this is a much simpler plan than my first, but I do love the complex intricacies of a good stage production. Ah well, enough of that, I will take those papers I saw you put in your coat. They'll be quite unnecessary now."

Hampton hesitated, glancing over at Jess.

188

"Come now, lad," Canfield insisted impatiently. "I'm sure you don't want anyone else here to get hurt."

Turning Hampton around, Canfield reached for the papers that were in the young man's breast pocket. Hampton stepped back. Concealed in the shadows, the narrow water trough running from the spring to the cabin's kitchen window had gone unnoticed. Hampton backed against it and fell backwards. Instantly his feet flew up and caught Canfield's gun-wielding hand before striking his chin. The sharp kick sent Canfield reeling backward and the gun flying from his grasp.

Momentarily stunned by the surprising move, Jess caught a glimpse of the moonlight reflecting on the shiny gun barrel. She quickly grabbed the gun and tossed it over by Hampton. Then she ran back toward the path to the village calling for Mac.

Within a few seconds, she heard footsteps and saw at least four men running up the path toward her. They evidently were already on their way back when she had called.

"Mac, hurry. It's Canfield!" she cried as he reached her side.

"No, Jess," Mac corrected as he tried to calm her down. "Melden says it's not Canfield."

"Not down there," she said breathlessly. "Up there, by the spring. Hurry!"

Jess followed them as they rushed toward the spring. Much to their surprise, they found young Hampton standing with the pistol aimed at the real Howard Canfield who was sitting on the ground rubbing his sore chin.

"Hampton?" Melden exclaimed. "But how?"

Jess stepped forward and smiled with satisfaction. "He was magnificent. He caught Canfield off guard by flipping backward over the water trough there and kicking the gun out of his hand as he knocked him down."

During dinner Jessica had noticed the superior attitude displayed by Melden toward Samuel. She found great delight in relating the story of Hampton's daring without mentioning the accidental nature of the feat.

Melden looked at Hampton in disbelief, but it was a hard story to dispute with the young man standing there holding the gun.

"And is that what happened?" he asked Hampton in amazement.

"Well, yes . . . quite so. The gun fortunately landed right next to me, and I simply took it from there." With a grateful glance at Jess, he took a deep breath and smiled with satisfaction.

Melden pulled Canfield to his feet. As he and Hampton ushered their prisoner back to the house, Jessica asked Mac about the men coming back from Sycamore Creek.

"Bear Paw and his men reached the cabin first," he answered, putting his arm around her shoulders.

"They got away then?" she asked.

Her husband shook his head no. "Little Sparrow got away, but Canfield—or whatever his name was—Johnson, and Stinson didn't. Bear Paw's tomahawk has finally drawn blood."

"You mean—dead?"

Mac nodded, "All three."

"Oh no. Do you think this'll bring the militia in?"

"I don't think so. When we take Canfield in, the whole story will come out. Stinson and Johnson were already escapees, and the man posing as Canfield was one of the ones behind the deaths of Quiet Bear and Tall Tree. If anyone is held accountable for their deaths, it'll be the real Canfield and the four renegades."

Hampton joined the couple as they entered the house. Ecstatic with the turn of events, he took hold of Mac's arm to get his attention. "She was remarkable! I say, such daring. Do you know she stopped and refused to do as Canfield ordered, even with a pistol at her back!"

Mac looked down at Jess and frowned slightly, aware of the chance she had taken.

"Well, I . . ." Jessica stammered.

"Don't be modest, Mrs. Macklin. I say, you American women do seem to be handsomely endowed with a generous amount of determination and spunk," Hampton went on enthusiastically.

A smile began to slowly appear on Mac's face. Jessica was quick to read his thoughts and declared defensively, "I am not stubborn. I just . . . just was tired of people trying to carry me off to places I don't want to go, to do me in because of this inheritance."

"Isn't she something!" Hampton glowed with admiration.

"She certainly is," Mac grinned with pride, pulling her to him and enclosing her in his strong arms.

21

The next afternoon, Mac sat beside his wife on the porch with his grandparents. He had just returned from Ellensgate after escorting Howard Canfield to the constable's office with Melden and Hampton.

During the trip, Canfield had told them the entire story of his activities. Far from being reluctant to confess, he seemed eager to have an audience to appreciate the finer points of his elaborate scheme.

"I still don't understand how Little Sparrow and Bear Paw became involved with Canfield," Grandfather Macklin puzzled.

"According to Canfield, the actor, Crane, came up here looking for Jess, and Little Sparrow was very curious as to why. Crane was quite taken with Little Sparrow and had some long talks with her. She's the one who gave him and Canfield the idea to encourage the discontent among Mitakiah and Bear Paw's friends. Just like Bradford, Canfield is a devious, calculating character and seems to really enjoy manipulating people for his own benefit."

"But how in the world did Canfield find Stinson and Johnson?" Jessica wondered.

"Unfortunately, Mr. Smythe unwittingly put Canfield and Crane onto them," Mac explained. "When Crane, posing as Canfield, showed up at Smythe's office, Smythe told him about what had happened at Sir Gaston's estate two years ago and why Bradford and those two were sent to prison. Crane reported this to Canfield, who thought it was some sort of poetic justice, I guess, that the two who'd helped his brother would help him. So he managed to help them escape.

"Seems Canfield has this flair for the dramatic. He planned the entire scheme like some production for the stage. He felt pretty safe in the knowledge that communication between Smythe and the museum in England would take months, so he had plenty of time to set up everything."

Unwilling to point out how his grandparents had unknowingly been key players manipulated in the elaborate plot, Mac ended his story before that fact could be mentioned. "I don't know about anyone else, but I'm starved."

"Of course you are, dear," Gran declared. "Come along, Jessica, let's see what we can stir up for our men."

Mac returned Jessica's smile as she followed Gran into the house to prepare some lunch, then he turned toward his grandfather who sat looking out across the panorama of valley and mountains. The old gentleman was in deep thought, and Mac waited for the observations he knew would soon be forthcoming from the man he'd grown up to recognize as an astute scholar, wise teacher, and keen observer of his fellow man. His grandfather didn't disappoint him.

In a few minutes, he shook his head and mused, "Every step carried out like clockwork, includin' the help from Little Sparrow, her brother, and his friends. 'Tis a tragedy

193

he could rely on those devilish tools of fear, suspicion, greed, and vengeance to create such an explosive situation to destroy the two people standin' in his way of possessin' that fortune in jewels.

"But, lad, success was right there within his grasp except for three things. In his madness, he never imagined the integrity of Quiet Bear and the others on the Council here or those poor settlers. His next big mistake was underestimatin' you and that sweet little bride of yours. But the most important element of all was the wild storm itself. The good Lord whipped up that storm to prevent both the settlers and our people from launching an attack on one another until the real story could be sorted out. I've seen many a miracle in my time, lad, but I never cease to be amazed by his masterful workin's.

"I reckon Canfield will be shakin' his head for a good many years to come, wonderin' just why his elaborate scheme fell apart. Pity is, he'll probably never come to understand the truth of it."

The next morning as Mac and Jessica were tending to Ettinsmoor and Lady, a young man arrived from Ellensgate carrying the monthly mail. With it came an envelope for Jessica.

Dear Mrs. Macklin,
    I wanted to thank you again for your generosity to the museum and your cordial treatment of a stranger in your midst. We are on our way back home now. Mr. Melden is returning to England by way of Vienna where he will meet an entourage of security men to transport the jewels to Cheltenham. I have decided to make a small detour on the way back to visit with a beautiful young nurse who saved my life.

Thank you again. When I am back home in Cheltenham, I will have some wonderful stories to tell my children about the remarkable people I met in a place called Iron Mountain.

Ever at your service,
Samuel Hampton

Jess knew she would not be terribly surprised if she someday learned that Samuel Hampton had decided to return to America for a while. Unless she was mistaken, the mysterious magnetism of a new frontier had snared another unlikely candidate. Mac agreed with her speculation about the young Englishman. She put the letter away and as they finished grooming the horses, they began discussing preparations to return to Dunston within the next two days. They were just leaving the stable when they heard a commotion on the far side of the village. It wasn't long before they could see a line of wagons and horses bringing the women and children back home. A messenger had been sent the morning before telling them it was safe to return.

To Jess, it seemed like it had been ages since they had left instead of only days. She linked her arm in Mac's, and they walked to the village green to watch the procession of returning friends. Waving to Oskati and Adá on the lead wagon, they followed along beside it until it stopped in front of their home.

Oskati jumped to the ground and helped his wife down before turning to Mac and shaking hands warmly. The two young men exchanged looks of glad relief, fully appreciating the joyful homecoming and the fact that further tragedy had been averted.

"Mac—" came a tiny voice from the wagon.

Little Sara stood there, her chubby arms outstretched. Mac reached up to the child to lift her from the wagon seat. She hugged his neck tightly and smiled at Jessica. Then she whispered in Mac's ear, "I think she's pretty too." He grinned.

As Mac carefully handed Sara to her mother, Jess could not help but think that someday before too long, her husband would be carrying their own child in his arms. She could hardly wait to joyfully share their news with Adá.

The men had nearly finished unloading the wagon when a neighbor called to Oskati and directed their attention toward a lone wagon approaching. Squinting into the morning sun, Mac recognized the driver as the father of young Thaddeus, the boy he'd rescued at the river. The man was accompanied by his wife and their two children.

After reining in his team, Ed McCullough jumped down and nervously looked about him as several curious Cherokee villagers gathered around. Clearing his throat and clutching his broken arm in its sling, the settler came forward and extended his hand to Mac.

"Mr. Macklin."

"McCullough," Mac acknowledged, shaking his hand. He then introduced Oskati and Adá. "How're things at the camp?"

"We've moved north and west of the river. It seems a good site.

"Mr. Macklin, I'm afraid we were so upset the other day, we couldn't say a proper thank you for saving our boy. So we've brought you something."

"That wasn't necessary," Mac said, a bit embarrassed by this public acknowledgment of gratitude.

McCullough led them to the back of the wagon. "I'm a furniture maker by trade," he continued. "Alder said you'll be needing one of these soon." He pulled a canvas tarp off a lovely handcarved cradle. The exquisite workmanship astounded Mac and Jess by its beauty.

McCullough went on. "I made this for Thaddeus before he was born, and our littlest one has almost outgrown it. It was washed up on the shore when our wagon was swept away, but it's still as good as new. We thought it would, in a small way, show how grateful we are."

"But we can't—" Mac started.

"Please," McCullough interrupted. "I know there's no way we can ever really repay you, but it'd make us feel better if you would accept it."

Mac took a deep breath and looked at Jess. He smiled broadly as he nodded in acceptance.

The couple then invited the young family to meet Mac's grandparents. They asked Oskati and Adá to join them as well. It would be a good opportunity to get to know the people who would be sharing their valley.

Two days later, Mac and Jessica said their good-byes. It was a sad occasion as they were leaving good friends and a loving family.

Oskati insisted they take his wagon so they could transport the cradle. He also did not want them to have to sleep on the cold ground going back. Their friend told them it would insure their return before too long to the village cradled in the mountains of the Shaconage.

As they rode away from the village, both of them felt very hopeful about the way the two groups in the valley would get along. Jess could almost imagine Quiet Bear smiling down at them from heaven in approval and gratitude that the promise made to him had been kept.

Waving good-bye, Jessica blinked back tears of parting. She and Mac both were thankful to be on the way home. In contrast to the anxiety experienced on the trip up, their return would be filled with the joyful planning for their future, for the future of their new family.

Epilogue

The young Macklin family would grow to include four sons and one daughter, all of whom would share in the exciting challenge of building a new nation. By the time their first-born son, Roger Aloysius Macklin, would reach five years old, their country would also have begun to grow in a significant way. In September 1787, the American states would have a new constitution that would serve as a successful yardstick for governing the nation.

Because of the difficulties associated with the large inheritance, Jessica and Mac decided to follow the lead of several other patriots by donating the reward received for the capture of Stinson and Johnson toward defraying the country's huge war debt. Jessica felt that Sir Gaston and Lord John would have approved, knowing how strong their desire for American independence had been.

Harold Smythe made the following entry in his personal journal after making the final arrangements according to their wishes:

I have, in my particular profession, the misfortune to come in contact with a wide variety of unsavory characters. By virtue of its vast wealth of resources, America sits like a tempting treasure trove simply waiting to be plundered by unscrupulous, greedy charlatans.

I thank the Lord for the pleasure of also becoming acquainted with young people like Andrew and Jessica Macklin who share a vision for this new land and will work with integrity and courage toward that end. God bless them and pray, increase their number.

November 30, 1782